kinch

kinch

a tally of unravellings

Laurie Evan Owen

Matador
9 Priory Business Park
Kibworth Beauchamp
Leicestershire LE8 0RX, UK
Tel: (+44) 116 279 2299
Fax: (+44) 116 279 2277
Email: books@troubador.co.uk
Web: www.troubador.co.uk/matador

ISBN 978 1784623 623

Cover design by the author and Naomi Green of Matador

British Library Cataloguing in Publication Data.
A catalogue record for this book is available from the British Library.

Printed and bound in the UK by TJ International, Padstow, Cornwall
Typeset in Adobe Garamond Pro by Troubador Publishing Ltd

Matador is an imprint of Troubador Publishing Ltd

'In my room, the world is beyond my understanding
But when I walk I see that it consists of three or four hills and a cloud.'
(Wallace Stevens – from *Of the Surface of Things*)

'He had bought a large map representing the sea,
Without the least vestige of land:
And the crew were much pleased when they found it to be
A map they could all understand.'
(Lewis Carroll – from *The Hunting of the Snark*)

'The Dust behind, I strove to join
Unto the Disc before –
But Sequence ravelled out of Sound
Like Balls – upon a Floor.'
(Emily Dickinson – *poem no. 992*)

contents

to E. M.

... sine qua non ...

tab: 1

which observes the man Pigeon in sporadic flight

The narrowness of the way took him by surprise.
Between wiremesh and logbark,

... coat, heavy,
flapping heavy
about his legs

... not thought...
... not seen...

... coat, heavy,
heavy, snagging
on fallen sycamore.

Clear. At last.
He looks back.
Makes his way
through grass.
Easy.
Laughs up,
oh yes,
into glare, heat...
The field is large and flat. Away to his left stand a pair of dutch barns,
open-sided, tin-roofed, empty, their fragile legs quite eaten through
by glare, heat...

1

He laughs.

Stops. Takes off his coat.

Regards the torn pocket.

Lets the cloth,

brother cloth,

slip from his hands.

... not thought...

... not seen...

Drift down.

This field. The parched spring is on it.

Couch grass is here. So is hairgrass, wild barley, wood millet,
the bleached ochres unrolling to a mile-long trapezium wedge.

The man is located with his back to a wiremesh fence. Before him,
beyond the field, stretches a rank of chalk hills, treeless but with jigsawn
clusters of black gorse scattered on the slopes – short grass, tight skin of
soil – the pale scars of four, maybe five, disused chalkpits –
the White Mark triangle, isosceles.

Drift down.

Drift.

Behind the barns, extending to the base of the nearest hill, is a forest of
young spruce, confined uneasily, at waist height, by a single-wire fence.
Nailed to each fencepost is a sign warning would-be trespassers of the
'strictly private status of the aforementioned plantation and the legal
conditions appertaining thereto'. If the man's face were not hidden by
his outspread hands, his nostrils would be able to detect, now and then,
the acrid whiff of creosote.

Uneasily confined,
and yet...

Listen.

Into the silence, at the forest edge, a seepage of low sound.
Halfway along its length, the greenery splits open.
Something liquid, brutal, curls out, is sucked back in again.

On the opposite side of the field, to the man's right, is a concrete levee
built to carry one of the earliest narrow-gauge Stevensonian locomotives
to a tunnel drilled into the soft chalk of the first hill. At this end the
ridge drops to show a glint of rail and beyond it a sky webbed in pylon
cables. Going north the track rises sharply before levelling out near the
tunnel, at which point the levee is far above the field, a grizzled thigh in
the migraine heat, sprouting sorrel and buddleia from its broken veins.

The spasm fades. The head lowers. Past his fingers the man sees a dim
savannah crisscrossed by chalkhill blue and brimstone and tortoiseshell,
an endless throb-and-shift of heat and honey-brown and silver.

Detaching hands from face,
he starts walking toward the hills.
Big-boned, round-shouldered, arms loose at his sides,
all about him the high tinnitic roundsong of the grasshoppers.
Bent forward, thick-necked, long-headed, bull-headed, hair a thin white
fuzz, he lifts his feet out of and back into the dying millet, savours the
hiss of it against his shoes, its whip and tickle on his hands.

The eyes are small in the oversize head.

Covering the right side of his face, from high on the forehead to just below the ear but entirely missing the nose, is a foetus-shaped purple birthmark. Elsewhere the face is wax-white, reddened only slightly, down the rim of his nose, by the long weeks of heat.

Hot all day,
but the day nearly over.
Midges smoke-ring his head,
but he doesn't mind.
From his left trouser pocket he extracts a tiny furl of screwed-up paper.
From the right pocket he pulls more scraps of paper and a block of roseate nephritic jade worked into the likeness of a seated monkey.
Breath clouds its surface.
The man's lips form a smile.
Or half-smile.

A fly crawls up the birthmark.

The eye wrinkles.

The fly drops off.

tab: 2

*which discovers the Dean of Axton and his Nurse, Clarissa Mockhardt,
en route to an unspecified destination*

Evening.

The Manse, grounds of same, approach drive.

An antique phaeton, slewing left, rains chunks of pink and grey on the mottled velours of the South Lawn. The carriage's two black geldings veer left once again as the gravel road turns back on itself to the Manse before straightening out to give a clear run to the Gatekeeper's Lodge. Wheels rip ditches through the crushed granite. The sole passenger, male, clings to the side, as his driver, female, on the driving perch, screams uninventive obscenities at the beasts below her.

The air streaming past the man's face is thick with flying ants, peppering his eyes and mouth. He wrenches his head around out of the wind, slithering off the narrow bench and onto the floor with one hand clamped to the brass rail above, retching and spitting as the winged bodies squirm their way into the tightest crannies of his maw.

Clarissa.

She. The Nurse.

Laughs and chews.

Reins wrapped round the arthritic lump of her right fist, she slashes at the geldings with the scourge gripped in her other hand. On, on she goads them, their withers stung raw from the bite of knotted leather. Buffeted, slammed against varnish, the passenger feels a qualified afflatus roll through him in waves. He spits out the last of the fat black intruders and

5

lifts a free hand to hook into the folds of his driver's cream and purple peacock-patterned frock. She swings around, baring in anticipation an implausibly pristine double rack of china-bright teeth.

'Faster you witch!' demands the passenger.
The whip cracks.
A deep-throated roar resounds over the din of swirling gravel:
'Gerron!'
'Gerron!'
'Gerronyafockers!'
His fingers screw into the back of her dress, clockwise, anti-clockwise, clawing at the laths of hot muscle.
'Faster, faster!'
He grabs at the carriage rail.
Hauls himself upright.
Five foot two. The Dean.
Forty-one years old.
Looks at least fifty.
The Dean of Axton.

Grey lids,
squeezed tight,
are almost closed.
Almost. Not quite.
His dribbling deadfish eyes
are fixed on the road ahead,

on something
on the road ahead.

tab: 3

which touches on the strange history of the City of Axton

East of the approach drive, the ground dips to a level swathe of pastureland, unnervingly green for these dried-up days of early May. This is the Water Meadow, which stretches all the way to the sloping west bank of the River Ax. Normally in full spate and forty yards across, the Ax has been shrivelled by the drought and its momentum depressed to a sullen crawl.

Up to their knees in muck and silt, a few jersey heifers stand at the water's edge. Their noses dabble apathetically in the brown sludge. One after the other they point their velvet heads toward the rumpus, adjusting focus, blinking off flies. The flurry of dust and trauma is far away. A tail lifts. A brassy twist of piss scorches into the shallows.

Beyond the river, along the high east bank, is a shelf of green lawn with a white bowls pavilion at its centre. From the near bank, groups of players are just visible in the shade thrown by the pavilion's backdrop, a sheer limestone escarpment which once constituted the formidable middle section of the mediaeval three-tiered Western Defences of the City of Axton.

Above the cliff, and set well back from it, looms a grandiose fortified wall, inaugurated in 1307 by decree of the Abbey Guild Governors. This was the start of an era which would see the local silver mines make the city rich to an extreme far beyond the dreams of even its most optimistic elders. Huge blocks of pink marble and granite were imported from

Ireland and the North. One by one the neighbouring villages were forcibly enlisted to hew and polish the great blocks and then to install them in the encircling shield of rosy ashlar. The grim generations of relentless weathering have barely altered their shape or colour.

Thirty feet high. Twelve feet thick.

The Blood Wall.

Legend would have it that the dappled pinkness of the stones was achieved by using the puréed corpses of the disobedient as a kind of ritual mortar. Preposterous of course, but many such fables have found root here, and not only, it should be stressed, among the uneducated. Tales surrounding the so-called 'Mer-Priest' of Axton, for example, are still discussed in a spirit of nervous postprandial levity by the city's dwindling *ancien régime* of academics and literati, even though that unusual cleric has been dead for one and a half millennia.

Along the top of the Wall runs a central gully, fashioned wide and deep enough to allow a double column of fourteenth-century Civic Guard to patrol with at least some protection from enemy missiles and bitter winds. The ten wooden watchtowers built equidistantly along the Wall at its inception have long since gone, all burnt down in one night by an angry mob to mark the bankruptcy and sudden closure of the last silver mine. But even without them, the ramparts still offer a fine view westward, over the Dean's plantation to the government-owned italianate plain beyond, with its empty hamlets, weed-choked lakes and wooded tors. And, on a clear day withal, so it is claimed by some, may even be discerned the ghostly grey caps of the New Malverns.

tab: 4

which observes the boy Kinch, setting an ambush

On the road. Ahead.
The crouching figure
is a boy of fourteen.
He rummages in the gravel.
When his fingers find a stone larger than the rest
he pulls it out. Rejects it.
Continues the search.
Lank hair the colour of old hessian hangs down over a pair of thick
blue-rimmed glasses. Either he is too absorbed to notice the hair,
some of which is trapped between eyes and glasses,
or it really doesn't bother him.

Carriage.
Horses.
Noise.
He glances up, frowns,
tips forward onto his knees,
wincing as jags of granite rake into bare skin.
He pushes his hands deeper, up to the wrists.
The pain is intense but still he works his fingers down and round until
at last his right hand hits something square and granular. Spreading out
his fingers, he finds the rough edges of the new shape, hooks fingertips
over the sides and pulls hard. It doesn't budge. Incensed by the
burgeoning racket of wheels and hooves, he extracts his left hand and
rams it down again into the shingle until it too finds an edge to grip.

He pulls at one side, then the other.
Sweat trickles into his eyes.
The shape moves, loosens,
is free.

He scrambles to his feet clutching
a damp maroon half-brick.
Unsteady for a moment,
he sees the phaeton and its occupants closing in,
draws back his arm, takes aim,
high enough to avoid the horses,
and with all his boy strength, hurls the brick
in a steep arching trajectory.

He turns to run, glimpsing his missile as it spins high, higher, into the
light; and then he throws himself toward the grass verge, arms windmilling,
feet flailing gravel, like treacle in a feverdream.

tab: 5

*which relates the consequences of the ambush and introduces Abel,
the Dean's gatekeeper*

Cleric lifts cleric face skywards.
Eyes lock onto the blood-dark lump as it flickers closer.
He guesses it will overshoot, which it does,
landing with a slap between the fresh wheeltracks.
'To the lodge, Clarr!' he hollers.

Moments later the Nurse brings the phaeton to a skidding halt between
two pillars of dilapidated limestone. The horses tremble convulsively.
She jumps down and strides off over the baked earth to the door of a
semi-derelict stone cottage which cowers back from the road, sheltered
from the sun by a family of mountainous lime trees.

She knocks.
And knocks again. Harder.

This time the door flies open and a broken bolt-arm clatters across
the flagstone floor. Feet apart, shoulders set, she stands at the threshold,
peering through the murk of an unlit room. Eventually she detects a
movement in the layered blacknesses of shadow.
'Matthews! Is that you?'

Out of the silence, a sound, a voice, thin and flutelike, floats through
the doorway and dissipates in the heat outside. From the darkest corner
of the reeking pit emerges a tone, a pallor, a bipedal protozoan blob.

Waddling towards her, a termitically fat giant dwarf emerges.
Short, like the Dean, but naked and completely hairless.
Abel Matthews. The gatekeeper.
In one hand is a large black key,
in the other, a large cut of bleeding steak.

'The boy's back!' snaps the Nurse, recoiling as the creature passes
between her and the doorpost to shuffle off out of sight round the flint
walls. She wills herself to follow. He turns the corner at the back of the
cottage. She stays a little way behind, pulling up a fistful of cotton frock
to pad her mouth and nose against the incredible stench.
The gatekeeper buries his face in the ledger of meat.
After a spell of grunting and snuffling, the neckless head grins up like
a gored cyst, showing her two pieces of steak in the place of one.
'There,' it wheezes, 'a little something...
to whet their appetite.'

Against the back wall of the Lodge and extending along its whole
length are a pair of connected lean-to stables assembled from sheets
of cement-scabbed builder's ply and scraps of broken furniture. The
gatekeeper lifts a blubbery arm to slide open a hatch in the upper
door of the first stable and lob in the chunks of meat.

A stifled howl is followed by a noise of bodies being thrown about, and
then a fury of hammering and scratching at the door. He looks up at
Clarissa, sound burbling out from an upper fold of his sweating flesh.
'Good as gold they are. Quiet too. Well, so would you be with your
vocal chords ripped out. Now the main course. Boy pie.' With this he
inserts the key into a rusty padlock, feels the levers give way with a click,

draws Clarissa into the second stable, and shuffles in beside her. After closing the lower half of their own door, he reaches outside on tip-toe, stretching sideways to the first stable to retrieve the key and lift the latch below it. He then slams shut their own upper door. 'Look!' he hisses, dragging her over to a slit in the boarded wall to witness the enjoined weight of two enormous dogs crashing through the door of the other stable and onto the path outside.

At first the ferocity of the leaping and twisting degrades the outlines to a mangled blur, but then, abruptly, the dogs separate as if wrenched apart.
Both stand motionless, jaws open, gasping.
The air quivers around them
as they struggle to readjust.

Clubhammer heads, tiny eyes,
flanks and shoulders disfigured
by a patchwork of wrinkled scar tissue.
Butterscotch mastiffs.

Eyes narrow.
Jaws close.
Lips curl back
on mustard teeth.
Nostrils confirm
what their instincts
have already told them...

Prey.

tab: 6

Prey.

Meadow-melt.
Becalmed in aurum.
Here. Always here.

At his back, the sun,
huge, squalid orange,
hung over pylons.

Before him, a scatter of beech copses,
and the Blood Wall,
glimmering mother-of-pearl in the low light.

'*O, Why must the Lady of the Moon...*'
Change settles on him like sleet,
'*...return to the loneliness of her Cold Palace?*'
grey eyes clicking from side to side.

A train whistle's screech.
The head turns hard round.
Chin grinds shoulder.

At the puce centre of his birthmark, the skin twitches.
The roar and the clatter reach a climax, fall to silence.
He knows what it is and doesn't trouble himself to look up at the empty
goods wagons as they pass by. He lurches into a gallop,
away from the railway embankment,
toward the spruce plantation.

Here.
Now.

Suppressing his fear of the darkening forest,
he lifts the single wire of the perimeter fence.

A squad of illegal volts
charges up his arm,
thumps into his chest.
He drops to the ground,
jack-knifing at the waist.

Pigeon. Quaint.
Discarded foetus.
Pigeon Cleary.

He raises himself
to crawling position,
a doll of jointed plastic,
doll hands buried in undergrowth.
The ticking in his cheek stops.
He moves forward on clenched fists.

Under.
Under the wire.

On the other side, the long grass gives way to a mattress of twigs and
needles and fir cones. He takes a breath. Springs to his feet. And drops
down again as the brittle offshoots of the lower branches stab at his
scalp and tug at his hair. Head retracts into shoulders. Eyes squint out
through half-shut lids at this new place.

The trees are in parallel avenues.
Above his eye-level the trunks enter a copper mist of fine dead twigs,
and then, above this, hang the first signs of life and growth, patches of
dusty viridian, dabs of sunlight. Only in the haze high above everything
can the firs be seen to fully luxuriate into themselves.
Diamonds of cobalt float from the topmost boughs,
relics of the day's heat.

Behind him.
A rustle.

Off again he lopes, body bent,
arms up and crossed forward
to stop his face
being ripped raw
by a zillion piny ice-picks.

tab: 7

which records the proceedings of an informal assembly chaired by the Dean's Nurse
and attended by four associates, including the enigmatic Brownie Turrentine

Farmtown.
The Silver Spoon Cafe.
Midnight.

A warm breeze insinuates itself through the slatted doors of the old kitchen. Junk chandeliers swing in a dream, trailing the filamented tinsel of some dead and long-buried christmas. Tacked to the yellowing walls at irregular intervals are vertical teak-look battens along which thumb-length pocks have been chiselled out to leave a queue of pale up-ended ellipses, heavenbent slugs, slinking through the umber varnish. Beams of charred sepia embed themselves into the rustic ceiling.

Ochreous.
Mock Alpine.

Smoke and fragmentary chit-chat curdle the air.
Clusters of men and women dressed old and cheap cling to the tables like grey fungus. A pair of white-aproned waiters move among them, sharing the occasional aside with a select few of their more favoured clientele. Most inmates are nursing nearly-empty beakers of a thick greenish soup decked with clinkers of burnt toast. Some have their faces sunk into large white baps overfilled with a species of skin-coloured sausagemeat. Nearly all wear hats, of no particular shape.

'This just won't do, poppets. Discretion's the word as ever, but if the quality and quantity of end product don't improve, then it's dark days ahead. For everyone. That's you too, Brownie. Most especially you.' The words are deep, throaty, female, used to getting their own way. The pattern of the speaker's dress emits a neon squawk from betwixt the braid lapels of her dingy olive duffle-coat, the hood of which is pulled forward to cast a baleful gloom on the face within. She continues in a murmur. The walls of the hood tremble. The voice grows louder. 'In the Grounds, too. Barely missed us. Cocky pup's even worse than his dad.'

She leans forward.
The table creaks alarmingly as her body is shaken by a coarse chuckle. She draws in a long breath, holds it, and lets it whiffle out again through glistening teeth.
'Abel's set the dogs on him.'
Nearby. A moan.
No-one speaks.

The tip of her tongue glides wetly around her open mouth, wetly around the room and its awed congregation. No-one, it seems, has heard. Attention is focused elsewhere.
On the wall. On the tables.
On the interesting ceiling.
On the state of one's cuticles.
A waiter stands motionless beside her, ready to collapse into a floury heap should she glance up and see his desolate victim grin.

'Lord above, Clarissa,' wheedles a scrawny flat-capped individual sitting opposite. 'What if this... I mean, what if it's just... a misunderstanding...?'

'Yes, yes, yes, my dear,' she sighs. 'What we have here *is* a simple misunderstanding, a misunderstanding of the word 'respect'. Psalm 74. 'Have respect unto the Covenant'. Work and Service being...?'

'The... er... Twin Pillars of the Covenant?' he ventures.

'And blessed are the meek. Is that not so, Brownie? Am I right?'

'J-just so, Clarissa. Of course.' Charles de Vere Bottomley-Turrentine, walnut-skinned salaried informer, of lowly but optimistic parentage, known to all as 'Brownie', whose mien and physique resemble those of a prematurely aged kangaroo, screws his face and as much of his body as seems appropriate into a conciliatory smirk. 'Of course you're right, Clarissa. With your... With his Eminence depending on you so much, how could... '

The hooded figure reaches her left hand across the table, takes a portion of Brownie's cheek firmly between thumb and forefinger, and pulls his head towards her. 'Now listen you oily weasel. His Eminence the Dean depends on no-one. I repeat. No-one. Is that CLEAR, sweetness?' She tightens the armed vice of her fingertips.

A runnel of blood navigates its way down his jaw. The hood is less than one inch from his ear. 'You are paid,' she hisses, 'for keeping your ears open. Not your fucking mouth.'

The fingers relent and with a whimper he drops back into the chair, pressing the collar of a greasy trenchcoat to his cheek.

The chandeliers swing and tinkle in the breeze. A peacock butterfly with a patchy portfolio of survival skills has found its way inside, out of the cold night, and is blundering among the plastic crystal pendants, dropping to the floor when it flies mothlike into a hot candle-bulb.

Silence.
The Nurse surveys her dumb dominion.
With every feeblest germ of circumambient sentience puppeted to the knuckles of her arthritic fist, she turns around in her chair and as though by accident elbows the waiter, still standing beside her after all this time, savagely in the groin. 'Oh I am sorry, Mario my sweet. No work to do?' Mario hobbles away, in extreme pain,
but only slightly bent over at the waist.

As if by inaudible decree the rumble of conversation re-establishes itself. Pipes and cigarettes which have been allowed to languish or burn out are revived or rekindled.

At Clarissa's table a new voice is heard.
'Plus ça change, mes enfants, plus ça change. Peregrinating, as one might observe, through this vale of tears and trouble, I never fail to be astonished by the obdurate...' – the new speaker is seated between Clarissa and Brownie Turrentine – '...and breeding like rabbits they are too. How many times have I been forced off our narrow pavements by some be-bratted pram-pushing squaw?'

Ecce! The Professor!
Admetus, Harold de Qincey. MA(Cantab).
The unnaturally suntanned face sports a long beard, wispy à la goat,

and a long cigarette, black and pungent à la Russe. Taller than the Nurse but lacking her bulky strength, once obese but no longer so, it would be misleading to describe him as slim since his attenuated skeleton is all too generously ruched with empty folds of fifty-year-old dermal crepe. But... *élégant, debonair, urbane,* are the words that nevertheless every morning trip bright-eyed and bushy-tailed to the mind of this cultivated polyhistor as he blissfully renews acquaintance with his reflection in the bathroom mirror. He too wears a hat against the chill night, a grizzled ethnically-inspired contrivance with large earflaps tied on top, all the better, presumably, to showcase his fine cascade of silver-grey tresses. 'For heaven's sake,' he concludes, 'one doesn't after all ask for much. Just a quiet life, a roof over one's head, a reasonably full belly, and a reasonably frequent fanny around one's doodle.'

An apprehensive titter circumnavigates the table, and then does it again, but this time stopping for breath at a pair of arthropod skittles seated on Clarissa's left.
'What's his name, Belle?'
'Whose name, my pet?'

The Siblings Dear. Tinkerbelle and Woofie.
Thin, stiff, clean, mid-seventies, their small faces are framed by close crops of fine white hair and surmounted by identical berets the shape and colour of dried figs. A smear of red lipstick on the mouth of the one nearest Clarissa is the only means of telling them apart.
'Whose name, Woofie?'
'The boy, the horrid boy, my precious.'
'Oh, him. I don't think we know.'
'We'll need to know, Belle dear. For the inscription.'

'Yes, to be sure. The inscription...' and, with a pencil taken from the snakeskin reticule in her lap, she scribbles something on a paper napkin.

Admetus clears his throat.
'Mmmm ... How about this?...
  For...umm... Blankety Blank Blank,
  Whose sad and untimely death
  Was a breakthrough in the art of
  Convenience dog food preparation.'
A smirk fidgets in one and then the other corner of the Nurse's mouth.

Tinkerbelle looks up.
Smiles sweetly across the table.
'Yes, Professor. Followed, perhaps, by this...
  He died so very young
  And o so very tender,'
Her companions clamp their mouths shut. Cheeks balloon. Eyes dilate. Clarissa and Brownie are chewing, with considerable difficulty, on handbag-size baps. The little sister smiles some more, and continues...
  '*We didn't need to chop him up*
  And put him in a blender.'

Too much. A soup mug crashes to the floor. The air teems with particles of slobbered bread and sausage-meat. The Nurse beats her forehead and fists on the table, feet drumming dementedly on the wooden deck. Brownie's entire head crimsons in pre-eruptive engorgement. Woofie and Tinkerbelle pogo up and down on their bony bottoms, hands folded, shrieks of glee forcing an exit through the puckered sphincters of their embouchure. The fingers of Harold de Quincey Admetus are stretched crabwise over his polyhistorical phizog in an effort to hide its delinquent convolutions. He cannot, however, hide the jowls, four sagging fatless flaps of turkeyskin, which normally hang in Corinthian symmetry from either side of his be-whiskered jaw, but which are now swinging exuberantly in all directions like rubber sheets in a gale.

Time stalls.
The waiters move in,
cleaning, sweeping,
re-instating.

Brownie stands up.
To stretch his legs.
To rest his eyes he looks over the assembled heads, through the smoke and chandeliers, to the main window which extends from dado to ceiling across the whole width of the cafe. Before the window grow lemon-scented oakplants supported by a trellis of split bamboo and knotted string. On the window itself lies a frost of condensation, marbled with drips and smears.

He feels faint, scotched by light,
the light from the streetlamp opposite,
its halogen heart beaten and crushed
into the plate glass of the window.
A door opens in the wall to his right.
Silhouetted against the dark night lours a man in a pale lab-coat, his arms crossed, hierarchical contempt written in the tiltback of his head. His breast pocket carries the initials 'G.G.', emblazoned green on a yellow triangle. The night foreman, from the glove factory next door.

Gridmore Gloves.
An old-fashioned firm.
With old-fashioned values.

The old-fashioned nightshift gets to its feet and begins shuffling back to work, a process not helped by the foreman's reluctance to give up his place of authority in the doorway. Carefully avoiding contact, the workers squeeze out one by one. The ubiquitous grey of clothing and headgear is the factory uniform. Over each worker's heart and on the instep of each slippered foot is the factory's green and yellow triangle.

A draught of night air chills the side of Brownie's face.
Someone is standing next to him, pulling his sleeve.
One of the workers.
A woman's voice finds its way through a cloud of grey tulle.
'Turrentine,' it whispers.
He feels something slipped into his pocket. Turning towards the woman, he catches the briefest glint of two olive-black eyes. And then gone, absorbed into the dwindling ruck of grey around the door.

The incident has passed unnoticed by his companions. So. Let it be. Whatever rubric lies among the screwed-up detritus of his coat pocket, it can stay there, til later. He lowers himself into his seat.

Apart from the Nurse's group there are now only three other customers in the cafe, each conspicuously alone at a bare table. In quick succession they each settle their bill and hurry out.

Clarissa stands. 'Time to go, darlings. We're keeping Mario and his compadres from their beds. And far be it from me,' she leers, 'to come between a wop and his beloved right hand.' The wops in question are tidying up with a loud and pointedly disruptive clatter, scurrying to and fro between the tables with perilous towers of crockery.

All rise to their feet.
Led by the Nurse, they thread their way through the furniture, stopping briefly as she aims a hooking tripkick toward the ankle of Mario's fellow waiter. It fails to connect, but she is too bored to follow it up.

'Goodnight sweet boys.
See you in your dreams.'

tab: 8

in which is set forth a sombrely 'monastic' vignette

1 a.m.
A wood.
Brand new moon.
No useable light.

Under the trees,
on the bestial floor,
atrophy unglues.

Through a snarl of brambled bracken
flickers a dull blench of concrete,
here and there, in patches.
A forester's silo.

Inside the damp bunker,
beneath rancid blankets,
a man and boy sit huddled for warmth.

The boy sleeps.
The man's eyes are wide open,
straining, making shapes
from the dark.

tab: 9

in which Brownie learns what was slipped into his pocket

1 a.m.
Another dark space.
Another low roof.

Tiger Street. Axton.
Brownie Turrentine.
In his rented room.

Behind him hang the tools of his trade, conspiring in the green light, tenanted to the walls by hooks and rusty nails. A cosmopolitan community of wigs, all tagged and labelled, is interspersed among a disorderly rabble of weaterbeaten hats and caps, in addition to five wooden crutches, a leg-brace, a box of walking sticks, a unicycle, a dismantled zimmer-frame, a tangle of trusses and girdles, an apron of pocketed leather filled with spectacles and eye-pieces, and a velcroed Quasimodo hump. To his right runs a deep shelf, one half set aside for exotic juggling equipment and the remainder piled high with contraptions, the purpose or purposes of which is not or are not immediately apparent. Still to his right, the nearest corner of the attic room has been commandeered by a disparate scratch-band of battered musical instruments comprising two-and-a-half acoustic guitars and an electric Gibson, a hurdy-gurdy, a bodhran, a stringless mandolin, a psaltery, a brace of bongos, a set of penny whistles and an Indonesian angklung. To the rear, hung up or set back in goodish order under the long shelf, and inherited from what Brownie can only surmise to have been an autoerotically-inclined previous occupant of the room, are the mirrors; mirrors plain and mirrors fancy, mirrors etched and tinted, mirrors magnifying, telescopic, cantilevered, and, in the reflective crystalline heart of the whole glimmery tableau, an opulent full-length golden-ivy-framed brass-castored mirror-to-mirror-to-mirror triptych.

All of the above collection occupies the entire available surface-space of three of the four walls. The remaining wall is hidden by a cavernous open wardrobe containing a hoard of hangered vestments of indeterminate age and salubrity.

He is sitting at a narrow writing table before a whimsically designed circular window. Its rippled panes and green glazing bars are arranged in the form of a hollow-hubbed cartwheel, which during the day gives the unobserved observer a perfect view of the adjacent alleyway. Even at this hour the streetlamp attached to the blank wall facing him still throws its disc of gaudy turmeric on the cobbles below.

Reaching to his left, he switches on a desk lamp, props a shaving mirror against its bent leg, unbuttons his coat and extracts a small polythene tobacco pouch from an inside pocket. In the pouch he finds a tightly folded square of newspaper torn from an Axton Gazette dated three years ago, one of a series of half-page articles presented under the title 'Famous Folk Past and Present'.

He starts to read, silently mouthing each word, but now and then breaking out into a soft kazoo-like hum......

tab: 10

in which the curious cutting is perused

......'dzz dzz dzzzz, dzz dzz dzzzz,

dzz dzz dzz, dzz dzz dzz dzzzz'......

PRUDENCE 'PRIMROSE' JENKINS

Of those poor and disabled buskers who were once such a picturesque feature of our city streets, there was one whose outstanding qualities set her apart from the others. Prudence Jenkins, known as 'Primrose' due to her custom of wearing a wide-brimmed straw hat decorated all around with silk primroses, had been playing the concertina on the streets of Axton for over three decades by the time of our interview. She was blind, and during that period had worked with seven guides and worn out more than a dozen instruments.

......'Ha, ha, ha. He, he, he'......

Her cheerfulness, considering her mode of life, was exemplary. A devout church-goer, she was renowned for her kindness. Many have testified to seeing her unobtrusively distribute small gifts of money amongst the poorest wretches of the street, who in truth can have been little poorer than the blind benefactress herself. Her devotion to her guide was also most touching. If a cup of tea was given to them during the day's round, she would turn to the young woman who led her about, and ask, 'Are you comfortable, Lizzie?', or 'Is your tea to your liking, Lizzie?'

......'Ha, ha, ha. He, he, he,

Li'l brown jug, don' I love thee'......

What follows is the story of her life, as dictated to the Gazette, in her own words:-

29

"*I was born March the fourth 1906 over a small draper's shop opposite The Black Swan, just off Towne Street. Father was a joiner and mother made artificial flowers. When I was just a few hours old, and even though it was bitter cold and windy outside, the midwife took me from my warm cot and carried me to an open window to show some neighbours how like I was to father. But the wind blew grit into my eyes and they became sore and infected. The infection got worse but mother had to start back at work regardless, and so it was I was put out to wet-nurse when I was barely a week old. By that time my eyes were very bad. My parents couldn't afford a doctor but the wet-nurse knew about this special eye ointment made up from mashed herbs and goat's milk and stuff. So she mixed it up and put it on, but she must have done it wrong because when mother came for me after work I was in a terrible state and my eyes were ruined. So that was that. I never saw again. She did it for the best, poor woman, and it was no fault of hers, and I'm sure I bear her no malice for it. But it meant I was kept indoors nearly all the time with no schooling except for what I picked up at church. Until mother passed away, that is.*

......'Knees up, Muvver Brennn,

Knees up, Muvver Brennn'......

"*Sixteen years old I was when she died. And then off to the poorhouse, and father with me, for he was very ill at the time. And then he died as well, soon after mother. So then they were both gone, and I felt I'd lost everything.*

......'Under the table you mus' go,

Eee-aye, eee-aye, eee-aye-oh'......

"*I worked in the poorhouse till I was twenty, and got a bit of schooling too. A kindly soul there taught me the squeeze-box and*

I thank her to this day for it. Mrs Drench was her name, and when she left she took me to live with her so she could care for me and guide me about the streets, and then after she died I had her daughter Alice for my helper. She was with me many years and might have been with me to this day but she took to the drink and killed herself with it. Poor Alice. She behaved very bad towards the end. Whenever we earned a few bob she'd to take me with her to the nearest ale house and spend it all. Always flirting with low street men, till in the end she got herself with child. A boy it was, and a great expense he is to me still. One night she fell over and rolled into the road, pulling me down with her. We were both locked up in a police cell as she couldn't stand up for liquor and I was obliged to wait till she could lead me home. Cruel of her, I know, but she's long gone now, poor creature, and I forgive her. I've had a few guides since then, but none of them was honest like Lizzie. Wouldn't rob me of a penny, would you, dear?

......'Under the table you mus' go,

Eee-aye, eee-aye, eee-aye-oh'......

"Yes we're very tired by the end of the day, ain't we, Lizzie? But when we get home the good woman we lodge with always has a bite of supper ready for us to eat with our cup of tea. And yes, we've done the same round for years now. Many ladies that's known me since they were children give me something regular. One good soul in Ascension Square gives me three pound every week, and another allows me five pound a fortnight, so one way or another I'm very comfortable and I've much to be thankful for."

......' Eee-aye, eee-aye, eee-aye-oh,'......

Soon after this interview, however, an accident occurred which was to deprive Axton for ever of its beloved old 'squeeze-box' lady. One day,

crossing Seymour Street, she and Lizzie were knocked down by a lorry.
They were picked up and taken to hospital by the driver, but the poor
guide was dead and Primrose had her legs broken in many places.

........'If I catch you bendin',

I'll saw your legs righ' orff,'......

After five weeks she returned home, but the shock had been too much
and her mind grew weak. She continued to hobble about on crutches to
the houses of the people who had for years given her money, but in a
few months her physical strength failed her too.

........'Knees up, knees up,

Never get the breeze up,

Knees up, Muvver Brennn'......

So it was that dear old Primrose finally took to her bed, in a room kindly
set aside for her in the Dean's Manse. And she never walked again, dying
not long afterwards, so it is said, from a broken spirit.

........'dzzzz dzz, dzzzz dzz,

dzzzz... dzzzz...

dzzzz'......

'Huh!'

tab: 11

in which is encountered a curious kind of puzzle

Brownie lifts the cutting to his face.

Raw tobacco. Camembert.

Turns away. Lets it drop to the desk.

'Huh.'

The features magnified in the shaving mirror are unsettled by a frown. Fingertips pinch the skin at the left temple and, painfully, rip a wide band of sticky semi-transparent moulded latex away from an area extending from ear to ear across the middle of his face, beneath his eyes and over the bridge of his nose. The exposed skin is white like ox-tripe, stippled with smuts of strawberry. He opens a drawer in the writing desk and places the knobbled strip of latex alongside two others. Shuts the drawer. Scoops out a gob of cream from a jar marked 'Mieczeslaw's Remover', smears it all over face and neck, and then wipes it off it as a coffee-coloured slime, using paper towels torn from a roll on the wall.

He stands. A straight figure. Not the bent marsupial of the cafe meeting. Adjusting the lamp, he lifts the square of newsprint up to the hot bulb. The oblique light causes dark grooves to appear at intervals throughout the text, revealing the faint tracks of a pencil, used to underline an occasional word or phrase, apparently at random. Sitting down again, he re-adjusts the lamp, and with a pen chosen from a pewter tankard filled with ballpoints, fibre-tips and neon highlighters, copies down into a spiral notepad the underlined passages.

In sequence, he runs the words and phrases into each other to make
a paragraph of seeming gibberish.

*'poor and disabled / over three decades / I was only a week old /
sixteen / over / name and when she / over twelve / up in a police cell /
she couldn't stand up for liquor / forgive her / Lizzie / of a ha'penny /
week / ever of its old 'squeeze box' / rise from it'*

And gibberish it stays.
Backwards, he tries it.
Every second word,
every third, fourth, fifth.
References to time, age...
Maybe.
Maybe.

Outside his window the streetlight fades.
He yawns.
Stretches.
Two o'clock, by the watch he pulls from his coat pocket.
Sleep on it.
Unwinding a grubby silk scarf from the base of his neck, he walks to
the darkest corner of the room and disappears under a low arch.

Click.
A wedge of amber flaps onto the intricately stained carpet.
A sliding door rumbles open, followed
by the hollow gush of cistern water.
Taps squeak on and off.

The sounds of washing, toothbrushing,
eddy around the blind space.
Click.

Charles de Vere Bottomley-Turrentine emerges, no frills, clad only in
his long day-shirt. He walks round the unmade legless divan in the
centre of the room, toward the illuminated desk. Fingers resting on the
switch, he has second thoughts, takes up the pen, and in a weary scrawl
rearranges the underlined passages into a vertical column.

> *'poor and disabled /*
> *over three decades /*
> *I was only a week old /*
> *sixteen /*
> *over /*
> *name and when she /*
> *over twelve /*
> *up in a police cell /*
> *she couldn't stand up for liquor /*
> *forgive her /*
> *Lizzie /*
> *of a ha'penny /*
> *week /*
> *ever of its old 'squeeze-box' /*
> *rise from it '*

'Tomorrow,'
he breathes,
fingers fumbling for the switch.

tab: 12

which resumes a tale of rustic indirection

Earlier,
same night,
the first day.
Dusk.

A rhythm, rising up
through untried skin,
rhythms rising and falling,
a sense of mild disturbance,
rhythm, rest, rhythm.

Above the steepled spruce,
a blue dragonfly
waits,   darts.

Down,
down,
and
down, through wells of pitch,
down through the ripped suet
of the mantles of the boughs,

moves a milky phantom,
muttering to itself.

One foot crunches in front of the other, toe to heel,
track no wider than a handspan,
pigeon-steps in a rabbit track,
rebated through the umber chaff of the forest floor.

Pigeon it is. Lost.
Telling wishes to the trees
in the half-light.
'...pluck from the memory a rooted sorrow,
raze out the written trouble of the brain...

Aha!'
A wall. Twice as high as himself.
Big broken flintstones mortared together between piers of glazed
brick. He leans on the chipped silica, finds a smooth round stone,
lays a cheek on its coolness.
'...graceful and dainty, ...among flowers,
green-bloused and long-gowned she was,
...though ...in his heart... '

He moves back and off again, keeping the wall close, close enough to
reach out and skim the hacked pelt with the palm of his hand. But then
the base of the wall disappears under a drift of ivy, causing him on
occasion to break away and dodge among the trees until he can find a
way back to the shelter of the flint. In front of him the wall bends away
to the right, with very little of its length visible at any time, even when
the brush and ivy drive him out into the conifers. Despite the gloom,
he would see well enough were it not for the woven mist of dead twigs.

Catching his foot
in a root-loop, he
stumbles, crashes
four-legged daft
onto hands and knees.

Looks up, round.

Under a low branch ceiling
tunnels of oleaginous spruce
scuttle away from the centre,
each one to its own dark pit.
At the furthest edge of visibility
a brown wraith flits from pit to pit,
no sooner seen than gone,
the air trembling in its wake.

Upright once more, he glimpses
something over his left shoulder,
and turns, and sees
the dregs of the dusk
                    winking at him
                    in red-gold stars.

tab: 13

in which Pigeon meets Kinch and they escape from a bloody skirmish

Pigeon-feet resume,
same night, first day,
tramp, tramp,
through dusk and brush.

'All hail, Macbeth' – a crooked beech tree, thick, stunted, ancient,
its branches beckoning, through the murk – *'All hail, Macbeth.'*

Further on.
A narrow door,
in the flint wall.
He accelerates
towards it.
Slows down.

Stretches out a hand, to push it open.
The boards are tongue-and-grooved, stone-grey with age. He recoils in
bewilderment as the timbers are shaken by a violent battering from the
other side. A bolt screeches. The door moves,
is forced open, blocks on a turf.
The fingers of two small hands appear,
curling round the doorside,
pulling at the ragged boards.
'Open! Open! Please!'

Behind the cries of anguish, Pigeon hears an eruption of hoarse barks, growing louder, nearer. He lunges forward, throwing shoulder to door, legs bent, thighs straining, feet digging dirt. He straightens. Raises right foot to waist height, placing it near the doorhandle, just above the small fingers. With both hands he grips the jamb, pushing at the boards with his foot, pumping muscle til his face bloats purple. Slowly, to the sound of splintering, the gap widens until the blockage gives way and the door bursts open.

A diminutive blur scrambles under the bridge of his leg, followed by a growling knot of animal muscle so big and heavy it strikes his foot up off the door. He drops to his knees. The door swings shut, as if on a spring.

He looks up to see a boy and giant mastiff locked in a deadly game of tag, round and round the trunk of the crooked beech.

The dog leaps first one way then the other,
each new movement echoed instantly by the boy.
Now it stops. The lips peel back.
From some inner cavity of its gut
breaks a cracked sibilance.

And then the leap.
But this time the beast doesn't stop as its prey slips from sight round the tree, but pitches and skids on and on, in the same direction. Eventually its jaws find the boy's foot – just as he is lifting himself out of reach, arms hooked over the lowest branch. Sharp teeth tear at the heel of his rubber boot, which slips off and is tossed aside in disgust.

The creature leaps again.

In the exact moment that its incisors close on the boy's foot
a broken-off branch rips across the dog's back.

The long body twists in the air like a severed worm.

Pigeon stands back with the branch held out before him. Lifting it
two-handed, he swings again. The dog jumps sideways, away from the
blow. As soon as its paws touch ground the hind legs bend in order to
catapult its enormous bulk effortlessly at the man's head.

Dropping the branch, he raises both arms to protect himself. Fear clicks
into rage as the canine teeth sink into his right fist. Man and dog crash to
the floor, writhing lover-like, side by side on a spongy heap of dead
bracken and blackberry. The mastiff's treacly incisors are clamped into
the muscle at the side of the man's hand. They roll off the heap, over and
over back towards the crooked beech in a spindrift of needles, coming to
rest on a patch of bare earth, hard and dry and ruckled with roots. In a
surge of fury, Pigeon tenses and heaves himself on top of the beast,
pressing down on its throat with his free forearm. With pain thrashing
through him, he pushes and screws the bitten fist between the dog's teeth
until his whole hand is inside its mouth. Roaring with the pent rancour
of his whole life, he pulls up the grinning head by the tongue and
punches his trapped fist to the ground again and again, forcing the
molars up past the wrist, knuckles wedging deep into the gullet, muscles
stiff, pushing, pushing into the hot gargling meat.

How many seconds... minutes...

Strength leaks like petrol from the great mastiff. Breath wheezes to
nothing. Spasms of resistance grow fainter until the body is little more

41

than a lax contraption of offal and bone. Blood from Pigeon's flesh dribbles from the mouth, down past a puppyish ear, and onto the forest floor.

'Help, over here,' Pigeon calls out.
The boy hobbles across and prises open the huge jaws. The man eases out his mangled forearm, which by now is quite numb. Shivering, he unbuttons his shirtsleeve and rolls it back to the elbow. When he sees the state of Pigeon's arm, the boy pulls off his own denim jacket and T-shirt, and then struggles out of an undervest, so worn-thin with age that it rips coming off his shoulders. Using his teeth for pliers, he tears the cotton of his vest and shirt into strips, and then binds the wounded arm as tightly and quickly as he can, finishing off with a bow at either end.

'That's very good, Kinch Wilkins. Neat, too.'
'How d'you know my name?'
'Seen you around. And your dad. Bad lot, he was. So they say.'
'Yeah. I know what they say.'
'How's the foot? Put your jacket on and let's have a look.'
The boy slips on his jacket,
peels down a dirty sock,
wincing as it passes over the heel.
Lifting the small foot by the ankle, Pigeon peers intently through the gloom at the white scrape-marks. 'Skin's not broken – you'll be all right. Stay here. I'll get your boot.'

Dizzy, stomach in knots, the man reels over to the beech, spots the blue wellington under a coil of brambles and brings it back. When he sees Kinch with his face upturned sitting beside the dead dog, a fit of shaking overcomes him. 'Chilly now, isn't it? Here you are,' he says, and watches with concern as the boy's sock is pulled on and the foot rammed into the depths of the rubber boot.

Kinch glances up with a shy grin. 'It's ok, they're a bit big anyway,' he says, and jumps to his feet brushing twigs and soil from his shorts. 'What about that?' he asks, nodding at the dog.
'We'll cover it up.'

With the light all but gone, they set to work shovelling forest debris onto the corpse with their hands and feet. When the job is finished, Pigeon squints through the shadows, barely able to make out the wall and its narrow door. He shivers. 'We need shelter, before it gets really cold.'
'D'you know Banneman's Wood?' asks Kinch, 'There's a place there.'
'Lead away then, lad' says Pigeon, forcing a smile.

With a lop-sided maritime roll, the boy strides off towards the doorway and is about to squeeze through when Pigeon grabs his shoulder. 'Where's the other dog?'
'Dunno. They nearly caught me climbing the main gate, but when I came back over the wall there was only one.'

Together, they push open the door and pass through.
On the other side of the wall,
at the edge of the Manse Estate,
they stand motionless,
cold, scanning north and east.
All quiet.

From the main flint wall running along the eastern side of the spruce plantation, a lower wall, entirely brick-built, branches out at right-angles and stretches all the way to the River Ax to form the southern perimeter of the Manse Estate. The pair shuffle along beside this lower wall to a place where one of the long coping tiles is missing and the mortar has eroded to dust. A few bricks have already fallen to the ground. Using his good hand, Pigeon takes out more and throws them over onto the other side. With the wall down to chest height, he helps the boy up and over, and then scrambles over himself, cursing as he knocks his bandaged arm. They are now in the Game Park, a twenty-acre segment of the Estate set aside in the 1820s for the rearing of pheasant and partridge, but these days owned, managed, and largely ignored, by the Guild. Kinch hands the bricks back up to his new friend, who roughly reassembles them, high enough at least to barricade out the elemental horror that may yet be stalking them across the night.

Heartbeat on heartbeat,
they inch their way
through the starlit park,
towards the huddling trees
of Banneman's Wood.

The stars back off.
A cusp of new moon
kites clear
of the hills.

tab: 14

which revisits the sombre vignette

1.30 a.m. The forester's silo.
Kinch has been asleep for three hours.
And now Pigeon drops, uneasy,
his arm still throbbing,

                      into a kind of sleep.

But warm, at least,
under their rotten blanket.

2 a.m.
The little wood flinches.
Something moves through it
along its narrow veins,
a lumpish furred creature,
white blubber, two-legged in a sheep's pelt,
lugging a gizmo, clanking iron
against a marshmallow thigh.

A skinful of malignancy
fatmaggots around the silo,
dumps its load, disappears into the night.

3 a.m.
A metallic crunch. A whine.
A rustle of beechmast.

tab: 15

which oversees the early morning activities
of some previously mentioned inhabitants of Axton

6 a.m.
First light.

Over fields silvered by frost a lone goose glides,
cranking the stiff machinery of its wings,
wheeling on a whim toward the blue rooftops.

The river's swirl, the chapped ashlar of the Wall,
isolate the buildings with a cold caress.
Tiny black spiders move along the streets,
the early shift on its way to work,
the late shift going home.

Old Town,
mediaeval still,
suckered to rote and praxis.

The University stirs, snug in its all-male corner of the demesne called
Jericho. The Colleges, Pusey, Augustine and Sacred Heart, were built
in the seventeenth century on three equal sections of a triangular plot
of land donated to the city by the Abbey Guild with the aim of making
Axton not only a forcing bed of Anglo-Catholic Resurgence but
eventually the International Centre for Constantinian Theology.
High ambition!

Cruelly dashed!

For centuries the student timetable has sandwiched prayer with study and study with prayer – Chapel twice daily in addition to the evening rites of the Axton Mass, with its potions and passes and oh-so-lengthy disquisitions on the subtleties of Sin (Mortal and Venial) and Punishment (Hellish and Purgatorial). Rich fare, indeed! But piety and intelligence make disobliging bedfellows, and the calibre of the student intake has long since declined to the *de facto* exclusion of all but the guilt-riven, the gullible, and the fee-paying no-hopers. But, Male! Male to a Man! And such Warmth! Such Passion! Such Comradeship! Such a Family in Christ! Such a blest self-provider of all its professors, all its lecturers, all its bursars, its porters, its cooks, and even (Domine! Domine!) not a few of its 'wives'.

The Vice-Chancellor of this doughty enterprise, Professor Harold Admetus, takes the air at his window, looks up at the opaline sky, sees a greylag goose, gliding, gliding over the twin-towered Barbican of Peter's Gate, banking east over Pusey's quadrangle. Jowls a-tremble, nostrils agape, eyelids sedately convening, this most sentient of academics becomes the subject of numerous poetical fancies
of the moist epic/lyric variety.

Grey goose, grey goose.
Wingbeats set to slow thump.
Adagio, ma non troppo.
Thump, creak. Thump, creak.
Oars of Theban trireme,
cruising speed.
Dipping low now.
Cathedral spires to the right.

And beneath, Trebizond Close, a cluster of tall-chimneyed cottages hemmed in by a tartan ribbon of green lawns and freshly dug flower beds. Still owned by the Archbishop, these dwellings once sheltered, rent-free, the kith and kin of the lowliest church functionaries, in addition to a meagre interspersion of dirt-poor widows, all selected for their humility by the stern officers of the Guild. But now... bijou abodes every one! And, behind the tuckered ruche curtains of an upper window belonging to the most desirable of these *most* desirable domiciles...
The twin-bedded boudoir of the Siblings Dear!

A pair of elegant mini-four-posters in lightly sandblasted Moroccan pine are cosseted in swathes of star-figured brocatelle, crowned with frilled and rosetted pelmet-valances, and attended by finely carved bedside vanity units. Subtly complementing the hand-blocked daffodil wallpaper is an artfully stippled ivory ceiling, prick-stencilled with cerulean forget-me-nots. And finally, *comme coup de grâce*, the lavishly pleated Austrian drapes at the leaded window are lent a *soupçon*, just a *soupçon*, of aery joie de vivre by an ingenious flying-prawn motif dispersed with wit, flair and panache across the lychee jardinière nets. Elysian. Truly. And. Neath sheets of pure silk.
Neath blankets of oatmeal brushed cotton.
The White, the Charming, the
Peacefully Snoring Anatomies
of Woofie and Tinkerbelle.

Grey goose, grey goose.
Neck in a sleek spear.
Streaming straight now,
over quaint-faced codcraft boutiques,

over preening moustachioed department stores,
over grassy knolls and Georgian terraces,
over stumps of charred Reformation brick,
over blue rooves, oxidised spires, gargoyles, graveyards,
industrial estates, slums in valleys, parks grown to wilderness,
and postwar semis grown to stuccoed porticoed Alhambras.

Grey goose, grey goose.
Sleek and streaming still,
now over empty reservoirs,
now pig-iron canals, now a prison, now a palace,
and now an orchard, a blossoming cherry orchard,
an exaltation of late-flowering pink and white blossom.

And now...
a small dark shape, irregular,
a chip of clinker in the foaming pink.
Human clinker.
And now...
a loud CRACK!

A pellet of rough lead
bores through the air,
splitting open the goose's chest,
wrenching the body up from its flightpath,
lodging deep in the dense red heart.

In the dew-wet grass lies a warm air rifle.
'*Diana*'. A cheap boy's gun. Anonymous manufacturer.

Black enamel barrel, chipped. Jaundiced stock. Worn trigger.
Fires lead pellets, miniature darts, sharpened knitting needles.

Five yards away. A duffle-coat, kelp-green.
Beetlebacked over a commotion.

Nurse Clarissa Mockhardt
inspects her kill. 'Hmm...'
She kicks the twitching corpse toward a holly bush.
It lifts off the ground in a balletic parody of flight,
misses the bush and lands in a clump of bluebells,
a painful but picturesque end to its short goose life.

Her fingers take up the wet gun and shove it
barreldown under a hot armpit. She moves forward.
The hood flops back. Hair clings to skull like foetal blood.
The ground thuds as her olive brogues stomp along the orchard paths.
Petals of blossom drop from the sodden lower edges of her coat.

A wall of yew.
A wrought-iron gate, newly painted.
With her arthritic right fist she fumbles among the loops and forks for
the small catch-lever. Finds it. Throws open the gate. Walks into an acre
of kitchen garden and along a grass dyke between rows of tomato
seedlings, through another gate, under limestone pergolas fleeced with
mauve wisteria, and out onto the broad forecourt of the Bishop's Palace,
home of the Stigmata Society. She stops to look up at the windows of the
fifteenth-century palace, moves around the corner to the path flanking
the east wall, and looks up again. All shut. Turns right into a gap

between the granite buttresses which in pairs girdle the firm fat belly of the building.

Head low, through the tradesman's entrance.
'Vive le bloody tradesman,' she chuckles.
Stone floors. A narrow black corridor.
Four flights of stone stairs. A heavy fire-door.
Crimson carpets. Walnut panelling.
Clink of china. Beeswax. Tulips.
And into a room.
Her room.

Good ol' *'Diana'* victory-rolls through the air and buries itself in a mound of cushions piled into the corner of a velvet chaise longue. Clarissa pulls off her coat, drapes it loosely over an armchair, and drapes herself over a soft double bed. On her back.
Brogues drop to floor, sole to sole
on the goatskin rug.

Her gaze skims the bump-and-dip of a gently botanical ceiling rose and sails across a lake of buttermilk to a fluted cornice,
matching the rose in its ribbed patterns of ivory,
lapis lazuli, and brushed gold leaf.

She lies mingled
in the bed's softness.
Silkthin eyelids glide shut.
At peace, the coarseness melts from her pale features,
the skin drawn taut by gravity over what is, in truth,

a delicate disposition of bone and gristle.
The russet hair, still wet and close,
frames the face in tender curlicues.
Eyes move under their lids,
pupil and iris rippling the skin, embossed,
decalled like price tags to their milky globes.

The heavy body shifts on the coverlet. Swaddled in girlish white socks,
the feet overhang the edge. The dress is calf-length, loose fitting, chinese
baroque on a field of jade. Blue peonies and red phoenixes dawdle
between stems of undulating acanthus. She dreams. The thick strong
fingers of her left hand slither over the coverlet, lose themselves in a
ruffle of printed cotton, come to firmness, roundness, warmth, scale the
curved wall, thumb leading over crown until the fingers fan out in
luxury on a quiet thigh, stay there for a while, and then creep upwards,
dragging with them the loose fabric.

The hips rise and fall, shift a little from side to side.
Fingers draw together, curling over cunt.
The right hand, in its knotted fist, moves also,
lured to the centre. The hem of her dress
is dragged higher, reeled in,
inch over inch on veined alabaster.
Rough-capped fingertips
sense their way under cloth,
meet soft inner thigh,
pull aside a stained gusset,
find, beneath curls of apricot,
the intricately flounced and puckered lips.

An easy smile walks her face.
As if...

Lento.
Lento.
Movement stops.

Down she drifts.
Lento.
Lento.

Into sleep.

tab: 16

in which the Dean prepares for a busy day

7.30 a.m.
The Bishop's Palace.

> *'Pange, lingua, gloriosi*
> *Corporis mysterium,*
> *Sanguinisque pretiosi,*
> *Quem in mundi pretium*
> *Fructus ventris generosi*
> *Rex effudit gentium.'*

Through halls of olive-washed terracotta it comes.
Past wallwide painted bas-reliefs
of mediaeval stag-hunts,
of bird-hunts, man-hunts.
Idylls of blood.

> *'Nobis datus, nobis natus*
> *Ex inacta Virgine;*
> *Sui moras incolatus*
> *Miro clausit ordine.'*

Past gleaming busts
of chubby-cheeked generals
and hard-to-please archbishops.

'Verbum caro, panem verum
Verbo carnem efficit...'

Over steel-cold chessboard floors it comes.

'...Ad firmandum cor sincerum
Sola fides sufficit.'

Past steel-cold nigrescent fireplaces,
louring over their preserve
like mobilised warlords.

'Tantum ergo Sacramentum
Veneremur cernui...'

Under hieroglyphed Egyptian lintels.
Over Azerbaijani rugs and Persian carpets.

'...Praestet fides supplementum
Sensuum defectui.'

Through the Greek and the Latin libraries.
Through lamplit studies hued by moorish
lunettes of amber and almandine.

And past the doors. Past the closed doors.
Past the sighing, the moaning, the heavy-
breathing doors of the Members' Apartments,
comes the sound of singing, tra-la... singing, tra-la...

A sweet baritone, marred only by
the merest modicum of vanity,
leavens the morning air.

'*Genitore, genitoque*
Laus, et jubilatio...'

The Dean stands at his window, transmuted by light.
Sound streams from the open mouth.
God is in His Heaven on this glorious day.

'*...Procendenti ab utroque*
Compar sit laudatio.'

Behind him a door opens.
A liveried butler slips into the room.
And waits, hands clasped, head bowed sideways,
little bird eyes locked on the singer's back.
Another bird-like face peeps round the door,
thinks better of it, and removes elsewhere.

'*A-A-A-A-A-A-m-e-n-n-n.*'

The singer is joined, an octave higher, on his final top-C, by the tenor
drone of an electric lawnmower starting up just below his window. His
hand turns the window-catch. A skein of water droplets shimmers along
the foot of each pane. Opening the casement, he leans out to see the
offending gardener disappear with his offending machine around the
buttressed corner of the building.

The singing mood still upon him,
the Dean draws breath, straightens up,
and steals unerringly into the first notes of a Tudor lament.

> *'Six dukes went a'fishing*
> *down by yon sea side...'*

He permits his eyes to wander at random, only half-seeing, across the Palace grounds. A sunken path. A cotoneastered wall. And then, winding lazily through its own spacious boulevard of turf and caked mud and amputated trees, the thick brown blood of the Axton Canal.

> *'... them ... a dead body*
> *... ... in the salt tide...'*

On the canal, a bargee family are enjoying an interlude of sunlit relaxation before roof-walking their barge through the Braddock Leyes tunnel. On the towpath a barefoot lad of about twelve is seated astride a big sorrel shire-horse and is twisting round to see his older brother doing something entirely mysterious (surely not cutting it?) to the mooring rope.

> *'... ... ... to each other*
> *... these words ... heard ... say...'*

The shire, a mare, is attached by means of two slack ropes to a bone-shaped wooden batten lying nearby in a pool of yellow powder. Also attached to it is the heavy mooring rope, which snakes along the bank, passes through the older boy's hands, dips into the canal, and resurfaces at the barge's prow, secured to a headbeam. On the flat barge-roof their father struggles to manoeuvre the boat with an impossibly long barge pole, while another family member sits behind him, head down, feet over the edge. Tied to the far bank is a second barge, with a crumpled tin chimney. Its only visible occupant looks idly on, elbows parked on the roof, crimson-hatted, and yelling what seems to be facetious advice.

> *... Lord of... ...rantham ...*
> *... ... the sea's ... away...'*

Behind the barges, an elm and a poplar strut arm in arm...
Oaks, and willows... A lock gate... And back to the towpath,
where a bare-headed man stands in profile, glaring at the sun.
Beside him crouches a black and white dog, a collie,
straining for the rapture of complete evacuation.

> *'O, they took out his ...*
> *and ... out his feet...'*

The towpath meanders back to the placid shire, where the young boy is still twisted around in the saddle, still staring in disbelief as his sinister brother cuts through the mooring rope. The large brown hat which perches on the back of the older youth's head, and seems full of something other than hair, is about to topple into the canal.

> *'and they balm-ed his body*
> *with roses so sweet...'*

The ground before the horse is blackened by the shadow of an over-pollarded elm. Further down the towpath stands another elm, pollarded to death. Both trees are part of a straggly hedgerow separating the towpath from the outreaches of the Axton Rugby Club, whose golden pitches and pin-bright goalposts seem to drift mid-air between the low spires of the Stigmata Chapel.

'Now he dreams twixt ... towers
but lies in cold cla – a – ay...'

In the exact centre of the nearest pitch, a small figure, beige on topaz, shambles away from the canal and out of sight, carrying a hod of bricks.

'and the ladies of Grantham
are pining a – wa –

– a –

– ay.'

With his master's song ended, the liveried butler executes a discreet *cough-de-politesse*, not in the least fazed by the gob of khaki mucus which sails between his open lips and arcs in parabolic splendour down through the split-beamed light to splat intact on a varnished floorboard.

'Breakfast in chambers, your Grace? Or in the Morning Room?'

'I'll come down.'

'Thankyou, sir.'

tab: 17

in which a childhood memory settles an unsettled sleep

8 a.m.
Pigeon.
Adrift,
in and out
of muddle, obliquity.

So, so long ago...
                              nine years old.
A church clock striking midnight.
A doorway out of the rain.

The day gone wrong –
the plan, the escape and the flight through Axton – the panic – and
peace at last in the hills and chalkpits – only to be seen and chased by
boys on BMXs – hunted, caught, and hunted down again – the word
passed through the tyke grapevine – the boys working in shifts – hunted
into nightfall – and then come the rain, come respite – but lost,
beset by ghosts and gall and his own worn shadow.

Midnight – the doorway –
'Come in, little bird, you'll catch your death.'
A woman's hand, gentle on his shoulder.
Scent of boiled sweets.
Fingernails glistening like globes of blood,
long fingers chunky with glass and plastic.
'I'll make us hot chocolate while you sit by the fire.'

La Doña.
Gown of sloe brocade.
Veiled, mantilla'd.
Velma. Meretrix of Axton.

*Come chocolate, come tears, and the dam breaking and the drawing
to her and the smell of marzipan and roses, and warmth it seems for
the first time. Drinking the chocolate in silence, in the lee of the
whore's gaze. And the little monkey on the mantlepiece, making him
smile. And then, 'You have it. Keep it. He'll be a friend. And maybe
you'll think of me and I'll think of you, and I'll know my monkey has
a true friend. So keep him, keep him with you always.'*

And she told him,
then she told him,
the story of jade,

and so he left with her umbrella
and her jade monkey,
and the rain stopped, and he returned
through the black morning to his prison.

tab: 18

in which the Dean partakes of a working breakfast

Stigmata Society. Morning Room. 9.05 a.m.

Rrrrrr-dubbadubba-rrrrrr-dubbadubba-rrrrrr-dubbadubba-rrrrrr-dubbadubba-rrrrrr-dubbadubba-rrrrrr-dubbadubba-rrrrrr-dubbadubba-rrrrrr-dubbadubba-rrrrrr.......

On a spiralling interior ribbon of lacy laurel green,
the brittle manicure of the Dean drums a roll.

The round onyx tabletop is freckled with a light snow of croissant flakes, the very next of which is at this moment detaching itself from the lower lip of the said prelate, soon to drop with an audible tink amid the harebells of a bone-china sideplate. Tight in its plucked chicken neck, the apple of adam pistons up and down as the last heeltap is drained from a cup of double espresso. Mouth compresses to a line and eyes crumple with distaste at the pungent niff of fried bacon, still lingering, twenty minutes after the other diners have left.

He is sitting apart from the other tables in a shadowed corner-niche of the refectory. Projecting over the niche and joined to the wall by three rods of wrist-thick iron sticking out from the back of its marble neck is an enormous marble head, a porridge-coloured Roman with a long rectangular face, fleshy nostrils and a powerful cleanshaven jaw. Empty duck-egg eyes extrude beneath eyelids carved like croquet hoops.

The stone features have been patched and repaired many times, but decades of diligent dusting have given the surface a sheen of adamantine integrity.

Behind the head and rising high above it is a large cross, constructed from two planks of dark-stained jointed cedar, bolted flat against the wall. Across the horizontal plank runs a sentence chiselled out in golden gothic capitals:

'IN HOC SIGNO VINCES'

Constantine!
Curate Emperor. Thirteenth Apostle. First Knight of Christ.
Hacking his way from York to Rome in a mist of heathen blood.
The dream, or Vision in the Sky (that one for posterity) – "In this sign you will conquer". Chiroi. On each shield a Chiroi. Chiroi over the standard.
In a field before Rome, by the Milvian Bridge,
the Proxy Nazarene raised once more the Sword of Slaughter.
And so it was that unwise Maxentius led his troops out of impregnable Rome, deploying them on open terrain, backed-up against the Tiber and no match for the Warriors of Gentle Jesus. Thousands of men and horses fell to their death in the deep river. Thousands more stampeded back in blind surges, some onto the narrow Milvian Bridge and others onto their own flimsy pontoon. The pontoon splintered, collapsed. Back, back they streamed, onto the bridge. Maxentius and his men were bundled over the low walls, plunging into spume and gore, dragged down by their armour to perish in icy roils of rivermud: – outflanked, out-thought, outbutchered, by a golden-haired braggart Apollo in a blaze of piety.
Heilige. Heilige. Heilige.

63

Seen from the central dining area, the gigantic head seems to hover an indeterminate distance in front of the dark wall-fabric, now advancing, now in retreat, an effect entirely lost on the burly brownsuited figure at present observed scurrying diagonally across the room toward the Dean.

'I do apologise, your Grace. A generator malfunction at the factory. I do hope I haven't put you out.' Spoon-faced. Balding. Chinstrap-bearded. 'I do hope I haven't inconvenienced you, sir.'

The eyes of the Dean, the eyes inscrutable of town gown and cloister, slow-ratchet-round toward the Managing Director of Gridmore Gloves. 'Sit down, Gridmore. Stop gushing.'

'Thankyou sir. Good news. Quarterly sales are bullish and we've excellent feedback from our primary outlets vis-à-vis the new Georgian range. Not only that but the continental operation's off to a great start, with the pilots in Paris and Berlin both doing well.'
'Security?'
'No problem there, your Grace, apart from the three dodgy kikes working the processor, but I think you'll appreciate the ingenious little insurance policy I've set up for that unsavoury trio. Springing them from the Sheds and painting them up for the warders' murder should be enough of course, but I had a brainwave the other day... and contacted the Leach brothers.'
'Oh?'
'Yes sir. What you might call a self-renewing weekly contract. The Leaches will undertake to deliver to the men's digs, on every Saturday morning, one finger joint cut from the right hand of each man's nearest and dearest, should the arrangement not be cancelled by me on the

previous Tuesday. All this for two hundred a week, plus the normal fee, when and if the need arises. It's a shame we have to use them, and a shame about the warders too, but needs must, and so on. Strong Commerce, strong Church... that's my motto.'

'Good,' sighs the Dean. 'Creech will peruse the books as usual, but I'm sure everything's fine. Satis, Gridmore. So long as the gloves do well.'

'No need to worry on that score, your Grace. It's the unique silky feel of them, so the reps tell us, and that seductive musky aroma. We simply can't make enough. Sweet Jesus! If they only knew!'

ssssssSSTCH!
Stiff claw of cleric
rakes air, rakes
managerial flesh.
'YOU WILL NOT!' – on his feet, spitting over the table – 'You will NOT blaspheme in my presence! Is that CLEAR?'

The businessman slides off his chair, crashing to his knees. 'Please forgive me your Grace. I'm truly sorry, I really don't know what came over me.' With palms spread on the floor to either side of the Dean's feet, he bows low, too low, wincing at the press of patent leather on his forehead.

'This interview' disposes the prelate, 'is at an end. I will not have the Almighty insulted by a cheap tradesman. The report's fine but it's piss in the wind if there's no faith and no humility. Go now. Go.'

Thomas Aquinas Gridmore, flushed and bleeding, struggles to his feet brushing croissant flakes from the knees of his new brown pin-stripe. Picks up his brown leather briefcase. Bows to the Dean. Takes a few steps back, glances up at the image of Constantine, gabbles a pious platitude, executes the sign of the cross, and waddles out of the room with a large brown hankie padded to his cheek.

As the double doors swing shut behind him, as his naked pericranium dips below the rim of an eye-high surveillance porthole, spurts of laughter leak from a nearby serving-hatch. Haloed in sleazelight, three dark-fringed female heads move in slow rotation, grinning, turning away from each other. And vanish. And re-appear in the kitchen doorway to enter and begin clearing china and cutlery from the breakfast tables.
'Next,' bellows the Dean.
The waitresses fade.
The double doors swing open.
Là... la nouvelle...
The *nouvelle arriviste* sets a sweet-smelling nervous foot on the carpet. A pair of low-heeled shoes in pearl grey suede twinkle silently across the red deck, coming to rest under the stony beneficence of Apostle No.13, Constantine No.1. A white-haired chalk-faced cherry-lipped child-crone in an aubergine pillbox hat and a pearl grey knitted twinset, carrying in her pearl grey Gridmored fingers an A4 Black 'n' Red cash ledger. Curtsey for Constantine. Curtsey for the Dean, who lifts an eyebrow and uncurls a saurian smile.

'Good morning, Miss Dear. And how is our Directrice of Tourist Affairs this fine morning? Can we keep it brief as I've several appointments before eleven and today is a busy day.'

'Oh, 'deed, your Grace. And I'm very well thenkyou.' Tenore-contraltino. Blinkblinkbreathblink. 'With a' – reading from the ledger – 'daily everage

of 7.3 visitors callin' at the Information Centre, we 'port no increase for this ennum. Indeed we're four points down on last year, despite our ...'
As Tinkerbelle reads on,
the saurian smile dies,
the eyes inscrutable skin over.
'... and then of course it's the weather because by that time HEPPsolutely HEFFrythin' is aar fault. Call themselves Christians on the registration form but they're so rude we honestly think the bedmennered articles wouldn't know the Nicene Creed from the Kraan, or the Kraan from the Code of Hammurabi, or the Code of Hammurabi from the Book of Kills, your Grace... Your Grace?... Your Grace?...'

To her sudden perturbation,
the Dean appears to be dead.

'Ncchhemmm...'
- a cough – a girlish cough –
which achieves the effect of a small twitch in the prelatical mouth –
'... but anyway, your Grace, I'll leave my accounts on the table.'

Something pierces the cataleptic crust enveloping the Dean. His upper body is shaken by a violent tic. The smile returns, a barren relic of its former self. 'Thankyou, yes, Miss Dear. I'm expecting James Creech in exactly two minutes and I'm sure he'll agree with your calculations. Convey my good wishes to your excellent brother and God be with you both. Au revoir, my dear, my dear Miss Dear. Au revoir.'

One minute later, and...
'Morning, Creech, my good fellow. Do take a seat and make yourself at

home.' The recipient of these warm imprecations sits himself awkwardly down on the proffered chair, jerking it, and himself, toward the table. James Creech, cane-thin and jaundiced, Staff Accountant to York National Holdings.

'So how are we doing, old chap?'

'Very well, thankyou sir. And getting better.'

'Fine. Let's start with the bad news.'

'Bad news, your Grace? Well... T&D I suppose... The upholstery section faced severe competition last year with margins critical enough to cause a pre-tax loss, so on my advice the Board downsized the Design Floor, retiring the manager and bringing in a new graduate from London. I note the frown, sir, but I assure you he's very malleable. Otherwise, not bad. Overall company profits stable at two million, with beds doing well and general sales up on last year despite the current trading climate.'

'How about Utilities?'

'Creditable, sir. Water's come up smelling of... if I may say so.'

'Flippancy doesn't suit you, James.'

'Sorry, your Grace. Let's see. Yes. The new sewage disposal unit has brought in a nice glut of rental fees. Might be worth considering mass production, if that wouldn't attract too much attention.'

'But it would, my friend. It certainly would. No, we'll keep things as they are. The rentals give a steady return and it's all under our thumb. Half-a-dozen units scattered among the more pliable Local Authorities aren't going to attract anyone's attention. Gas and Electric?'

'No change, sir. Very sound.'

In such manner Creech proceeds, on and on through the remaining subsidiaries of York National:

St. Helena Properties.	*No change.*
Gridmore Gloves.	*19% up.*

True Cross Publishing.	*10% up.*
Greentrees Nursing Homes.	*No change.*
Plasma Supplies Ltd.	*67% up.*

The accountant refers frequently to a thick notebook, the front cover of which is ornamented with a picture in blues and greys of Peter Rabbit treating Flopsy and Cottontail to a Grand Magic Show.

'Any complications with PSL?'

'So far so good, your Grace. Expansion is obviously more sensitive than in our other companies. Technically quite feasible but... well... we await your instructions on that.'

The Dean leans forward.

'Listen, James... The Health Minister sees no harm in maintaining the present growth rate for another two years, but he doesn't want further expansion until security's radically improved. It's an extremely attractive option but would mean a huge programme of capital investment, most of which would go into building a new milking-plant, fully automated and underground. He's promised 70% of the pre-outlay, but even with lucrative frozen plasma exports to the States the risk still seems too great. Perhaps you could look into costs, as soon as you can manage, and come up with some projections. In three days, to be blunt old chap. Sorry to be a nuisance again, but we need a persuasive formula to tempt the Minister at next week's meeting. I'll be pressing for the Government's input to be increased to 90%, which would of course make the whole project more viable, especially if we retain technical and operational control. So. That's the position. Why Peter Rabbit, James?'

'Sentiment, sir. And discretion. He was an old favourite of mine.'

'Mother alright, old chap?'

'Very kind of you to ask, and yes thankyou, sir. She keeps pretty well.'
'Close, aren't you. Does she have your head for figures?'
'Goodness me, no, your Grace. That must have come from my father.
Unfortunately I never knew him. Mother says he was a fine man.'
'Well, give her my good wishes, and anything I can do to make her
more comfortable – just say the word. Anything at all. That's it for
now. See you in a couple of days. Bye, James. God bless you till then.'
'God be with your Grace. And thankyou.'

The Dean brushes the crumbs from his waistcoat. Stands up.
And walks, hands on hips, to the centre of the room,
swivelling around to face the head of Constantine,
staring frankly into the stone eyeballs.
He gives the Bow of Friendship.
Breathes slowly and deeply.
Wanders over to the serving hatch.
'Sarah?'

From the kitchen doorway one of the dark-fringed waitresses
pitter-patters towards him. Drops a curtsey.

He looks up to admire the Constantinian half-profile.
'You will be at Mass this evening, Sarah, I trust.'
'Oh yes sir. And the other girls.'
'Never mind them. Wait outside the Vestry door after the service.
Just yourself. I want to introduce you to my new private secretary.
And make sure you're properly dressed.'
'Yes, your Grace.'

With that he eases himself out of her presence, pushing through the conkerbrown double-doors and striding out into a sunfilled lobby at the foot of a short staircase. His gaze is drawn up the stairs to an oak-panelled corner of the main entrance hall, from whence scowls down the life-size spectre of Bishop Cerdic, his luckless melancholic predecessor. The Dean stands still, mesmerised by an echo of the man himself, a quality of terminal desperation which somehow survives the portrait's clumsy execution. 'You were a bloody fool Cerdic Blunderston and no two ways about it,' he mumbles. 'No two ways about it.'

A creak of shoe leather.

He pivots round.

Seated on a wooden bench under a row of arched picture-windows, backed by a flood of sunlight, is a handsome young man of twenty-five dressed in the loose-fitting red soutane of a Helenite Ordinand. A Child of St Helena in a trance of hope, sporting an exorbitance of prematurely grey hair, gelled, swept back from the face, and streaming in oily elvers over the skull to a harshly-cut boston at the necknape. Handsome – skin of pink velvet, shrink-wrapped in muslin – browless, small-eyed, fierce-eyed, peppercorn-pupilled. But Handsome. Winsomely featured. An intricately whittled *ballade de* bone/cartilage. Whittled cheekridge noseridge, whittled soapstone noseridge cheekbone, whittled nosebone. Mouth... well...

The young man stands.

The robe slithers into columns of fluted porphyry.

'Excuse me, your Grace. Watford Scales is the name. I believe I have an appointment with your Grace... concerning the post of Private Secretary?'

'So. Mr... umm... Scales. Watford... Regis... Scales.
You 'believe' you have an appointment?
Believe?'

'Sir?' A frown rumples the handsome forehead.

'You used the word 'believe' in a manner which would seem to imply
that your conviction as to the existence of the said appointment is less
than complete. This may have been an idiomatic device expressing
deference, but your readiness to use the word in this way might suggest,
to an individual more captious than myself, some vagueness in your
attitude towards belief in its true and Nicenian sense.'

'With the utmost respect, your Grace, my choice of this er... most axial
of words... was meant to convey nothing but absolute certainty, as I have
the letter of confirmation signed by yourself here in my pocket. My use
of the word in that context was arguably injudicious, but it was meant to
be understood in its most essential, most Catholic manifestation.
Belief qua bedrock, non qua supposition.
And I am a little nervous.
With respect, Your Grace.'

'You'll do, Scales. Start right away.
See the verger about a new bib and tucker
then wait for me in the Latin Library.'

'Thankyou, your Grace.
I'm sure you'll not regret your decision.'

'I'm not in the habit of regretting anything, Mr Scales.
Don't grovel, and we'll get along fine.'

'Yes, sir.'
The porphyritic column hinges respectfully at the waist and glides
away on nylon castors down a narrow corridor leading off the lobby.
The Dean uptilts his face.
High, outside the tall windows,
a family of misshapen cloudsheep
meander across their gridded blue field.
'Laaah...
Laaaaah....'

Lapels are drawn apart.
Two thumbs wriggle into
two waistcoat pockets.
Buttons take the strain.

Sotto voce
to an almost-whisper...

'....sanguinisque pretiosi,
quem in mundi pretium
fructus ventris generosi
Rex... effudit... gentiu-u-m.'

From the carpet's soft maroon
the secretarial footprints evaporate,
like rain on summer concrete.

tab: 19

in which Kinch and Pigeon make their way back towards Farmtown

Banneman's Wood.
10 a.m.

Kinch. Pigeon.
In their dank cocoon.

The man readjusts, limb after limb. Peers anxiously into the yellow light
sifting through the holes in their tarpaulin door. Glances down at the
boy's matted hair.
'Kinch,' he asks, 'You 'wake?'
'Nnnghhr....nnngh'.
He shakes the boy gently.
'Arright. I'm awake.'
Together they ease off the putrid blanket.
Pigeon grunts as pain returns to his wounded arm.
They crawl, crouch, stagger out under the lintel
to stand up blinded by the morning sun,
sucking in chestfuls of the fresh morning air.

The bunker is ringed by a thicket of thorns and bracken.
Looking for an exit, puzzled as to how they found their way here in
the pitch dark, Pigeon notices a narrow badger-track over which
tendrils of blackberry have woven themselves into a vaulted roof.
He grunts a few words at the boy and starts towards it.
And stops. A blockage. Halfway along.

Knee-high hillock, tumour. Corpse.
'Wait here.'

Still barely awake, fighting nausea,
he edges sideways through the thorns,
toward the heap of bloodied beige.
Closer. Is it...? Could it...?

No, not the same.
For one mad moment he pictures yesterday's dead mastiff, free of its
leafy tomb, dragging its zombie carcass through the night to wreak
righteous havoc, and then halted, only yards away, by the risen sun.

Or... it is the same animal,
genus dog, same breed.
But not the same individual.

The head is twisted back in spasm, but there are no scraps of Pigeon-
flesh dangling from its jaw. Leaning over the body, he sees the cause of
death, half-hidden by twigs and leaves, sees a steel man-trap with its
teeth sunk deep in the ribs of the great beast. The roof of thorns would
have forced it low, belly to ground in a stalker's crawl. Exhilarated, the
scent of its prey heavy on the night air, it must have sensed the
nearness of revenge, and overlooked in that sweet excitement a second,
underlying, less pungent aroma, that of its pack leader, Abel Matthews,
whose sweated spores would still have been clinging to the metal of his
deadly contraption. Who else but Abel would know the woods well
enough to guess their hiding place?

Who else would come hunting at night armed with such a weapon? Who else would be crazy enough to set its jaws in the pitch dark?

'The other dog,' gasps Pigeon, returning. 'Dead. In one of Abel's traps. He must have put it there last night, for us. He collects them... the traps... all sorts... as a hobby.'

'Perhaps there's more,' says the boy.

'No. Not even Abel could carry two. Anyway, let's go before he comes back to check.'

'But that's the only way out... '

'Don't worry. Just a second.'

So saying, Pigeon disappears into the bunker and returns dragging behind him the mildewed blanket, which he throws over his back and shoulders, yanking it forward to cover his head in a monkish cowl. Suddenly Kinch finds himself whirled around and jerked backwards into his friend's chest. Turning briefly to check the route, and holding on hard to his fourteen-year-old cargo, the man reverses into the wall of thorns.

Ten seconds of ripping and crackling...
and a tattered armadillo emerges from the thicket,
shedding its skin with a triumphant yelp.
Kinch grins and wipes the sleep from his eyes.
Pigeon spits out a wiry blanket-hair,
and grins back.

Side by side the pair weave their way between sunlit beeches. The ground is soft. The air still. They walk fast till they get warm, and then slow to a steady amble. On leaving the wood they come to a pebble-and-clinker path which winds like a speckled snake across a heath littered with sorrel and young blackthorn.

'What do I call you?' asks Kinch. 'Is Pigeon your real name?'
'Yes. Pigeon's fine. I like pigeons.'

Over the bushes and to their left, the Blood Wall glares its gilded brio back at the sun. The path follows the course of the river, at present hidden from sight beneath banks of sheer granite. As they amble on, the flickering vista through the bushes is joined and grounded by the intermittent stumps of a dry stone boundary fence.

Further from the wood the track becomes firm. Errant verges become neatly trimmed kerbs. Tarmac replaces clinker on a downward slope, channelling deeper between the grassy banks. High above them, hazel and hawthorn commingle to form a desultory hedge, the slim trunks interweaving at eye-level with the tangled undergrowth.

Turning a corner, Kinch halts and grabs his friend's shirtsleeve. Before them a pair of brown toads have crossed the asphalt track and are leaping up at the bank. Unable to grip on the dewy grass, they slither down again. The exercise is repeated again and again with an air of increasing despondency. Eventually the boy walks over to the exhausted creatures, slips a hand under the belly of each, and lifts them high onto the bank between two hawthorn trunks, from where they shuffle and jump their way riverwards. Pigeon smiles. Rubs his woolly head. 'Let's hope some giant toad does the same for us.'

They move off again. With the Manse and the Estate left far behind,

Pigeon feels himself drawn into a mood somewhere between levity and hauteur. From the hedgerow he breaks off a wand of whippy hazel, makes a few slashing passes at an imaginary opponent, and then proceeds to trace delicately in the air before him a series of arcane pictograms. Triangles. Stars. Sphinxes. Chimaeras. 'I suppose you know where we're going, lad. Because I'm blowed if I do.' He outlines a house with the magic baton. 'A safe house with breakfast and a bath would be nice.' The trembling point of his stick draws a bowl heaped with cereal, and then a plate of sausages and egg and bacon, with a mug of steaming tea beside, and then, finally, a large lion-footed bath.

'A safe house is where we're going,' says Kinch. 'Auntie Maeve and Auntie Stevie's cottage. They're not my real aunts so we won't be found there.'

'And where might they live?'

'Farmtown. We can cross the river at the ford. It's not deep and we'll hardly get our feet wet. Come on. We're nearly there.'

Having parted company with the Blood Wall some while back, and no longer doubling as a moat, the River Ax and its gully of hewn granite have given way to opposing slopes of flinty loam and the murky shallows of Braddock's Ford, which Pigeon knows well as the site of the Old Paper Mill.

Up until the late nineteenth century, before the light industries of Axton's upriver neighbours caused a dramatic reduction in its volume, the Ax had been a considerable waterway. At Braddock's Ford the river's eastward flow was partially diverted by means of an underground leat into the Millpond, from which a chute of glutinous grey water would pour along a secondary leat to power a series of four vertical 'undershot' waterwheels. These were connected, inside the Old Mill, to the Pulping and Cleansing Rooms, in themselves just a small part of a unique but whimsically chaotic system of papermaking devised, refined and financed by one Deacon Braddock, amateur engineer of great inherited wealth, great enthusiasm and a singular capacity for self-deception. For three anxious years during the mid-1820s Deacon's beloved project stumbled from breakdown to farce, from farce to catastrophe. Eventually, convinced that his troubles were caused by a freakish confluence of bad luck and good weather, the irrepressible tycoon abandoned the paper mill and turned his attention from water to wind. He started work on his Improved (Wind) Power Construction, which was to be a kind of gargantuan windmill, a six-storey revolving hexagon, decked with nine pairs of crossed sails, in three layers of three. But then he died in an accident, hideously torn apart during a primitive wind-turbine experiment. And that was that. The revolutionary windmill never made its way off the drawing board. All that remains now of Deacon's Mill are a few stumps of flint wall and, lying on its side not far from the water's edge, the rusty iron framework of a single waterwheel, for decades the occasional support of many an Axtonian hindquarter... as it is, at this moment, for Pigeon and Kinch.

The boy is deep in Roman thoughts. His heel digs a semi-circle of shallow pits in the pebbled dirt. At the centre is an arrow-head of purple flint.

Pigeon sits, silent, nursing his bad arm. He looks over the ford towards Axton. On a tiered knoll the two enclaves of the City sprawl left and right in self-absorbed calm. The Old Town rises high, but is almost hidden by the rosy upstand of the Blood Wall. To his right spreads the rabble of limestone cottages, industrial estates and run-down shops known collectively as Farmtown... a tide of lumpy gruel, lapping at the feet of its wealthy neighbour.

Behind his narrowing eyes,
ugly tropes jostle for position.
A legless pig siestas in viscera.
Porkpie-hatfuls of black tripe split open, give birth.
A million-teated turd suckles a nation.

A furnace.
And through the furnace door:
Axton.
On the furnace floor:
Axton.
Ceramic cold heart
in the smoking gizzards:
Axton.

Nausea stilts through him.
'Can we go, Kinch...
I'm not feeling too good.'

tab: 20

in which a puzzle is resolved

P oor and disabled /
O ver thirty /
I was only a week old /
S ixteen /
O ver /
N ame and when she /
O ver twelve /
U p in a police cell /
S he couldn't stand up for liquor /

F orgive her /
L izzie /
O f a ha'penny /
W eek /
E ver of its old 'squeeze-box' /
R ise from it /

Brownie is annoyed with himself.
Unable to sleep last night, he'd teased,
dissected the damned thing... forever.
And here it is. Obvious.

Talks to himself in the mirror.

Midday. He has been up for one hour.

tab: 21

which depicts a convalescent interlude with Maeve and Stevie, Kinch's aunts,

and Kaisa Strachan, a district nurse

Midday.

Arcady Row, Farmtown.

Pigeon,

clutching jade.

'and so it appeared to them –

soft, smooth and lustrous

> *like benevolence*

fine, compact and strong

> *like intelligence.'*

Convex mirror in a quoit of gold cherubs.

Inclines head, first one side, then the other. Opens and shuts mouth.

Lifts a hand to smooth down his albino fuzz. His arm moves. The shape

waves back a curved cutlass stump. He moves a leg. Nothing happens.

Slivered images shuttle. Soft female colours crisscross behind him.

Hands that have bandaged his forearm raise it again to remove a

bloodstained towel. Sorceress beside him. Kneeling. Nimble witch

fingers unroll the satin sleeve of his borrowed dressing-gown, replacing

the arm on its bed of cushions, reaching across to give his other arm

an encouraging squeeze. His eyes close at the pressure of the woman's

breast on his thigh. A taste of egg is on his tongue, a wetness of sweet

tea, on his lips. He leans back on the sofa in a daze of relief.

Quiet voices.

Talking about him.

About Pigeon.

One of the voices.

Kaisa. District nurse.

'Let him rest. It's not been easy for him...' then quieter, 'As lab assistant at the school, that's right...' moving away, '...like an animal, Maeve. I've seen lab-rats treated better. Drench was Head of Science in those days. Three years it lasted.'

'Yes, we did hear things.' Voice number two. Maeve – broadfaced, eager to please, younger of the maiden aunts. Border Welsh. 'Stevie picked up bits of tittle-tattle, working in the bookshop, didn't you dear...'

'Yes yes,' interrupts the nurse, 'there's always gossip. I wrote to the governors. But I needn't have bothered, for all the good it did.'

Stevie, frail elder sister, gives a frail cough. 'Saw them at Easter, didn't we Maeve, the boys, like angels in their white surplices.'

'Uh uh... I'll bet...' Kaisa, exhaling. 'The pubescent male is an odd creature at best... but these... Twice I was called out – once for cuts to the back of his head – caused by what, he wouldn't say – and the last time for acid burns round his eye. A booby trap, on top of his door. Nitric acid. Not very concentrated or he could have lost an eye. And how, I wonder, did they get hold of the acid... and who kept the only key to the acid cupboard?'

'Drench,' whisper the sisters.

'Of course. And the other staff weren't much better, bullies or cowards the lot of them. He couldn't take it any more. A few months in a private clinic, and then back to the Manse with the Dean and that Mockhardt woman. I was away at the time, and haven't seen him since.'

She moves over to Pigeon's sofa and sits down.

Small blunt fingers touch the bandage – so light he doesn't feel it, just sees it, through nearly closed eyelids. She leans forward to tidy up. Blood-soaked wads of cotton wool and filthy strips of torn-up vest are dropped into a nearby pedal-bin. Medicines, rolls of bandage and a thermometer are packed into a battered box-briefcase.

Weightless. Adrift. His eyes focus on a pair of knees, trim moons glazed in black. Slipping into sleep, he finds fresh comfort in the strong neck, the jaw's soft curve, the rufous waves of her bobbed hair.

She rises carefully, smoothing the creases from her uniform. 'He's had penicillin and anti-tetanus and a mild sedative. Sleep's best for him now, but when he wakes up I should think a hot bath is definitely in order.'

The compact body, barely five feet in its flat pumps, belongs to the Finnish-born District Nurse to South Farmtown and the Choir School, Kaisa Strachan, one of a team of three District Nurses serving the whole of Greater Axton. Her lean, clear-skinned, thirty-five-year-old face seems primed to wrinkle into laughter or outrage at the slightest provocation. Taking a notepad from her hip pocket, she pencils a line of hurried shorthand and scowls at her watch.

Behind the sofa, two pairs of spectacled green eyes look on. 'Kinch is sleeping too,' says Maeve. 'Stevie's been up to see him, haven't you dear.' Stevie says nothing and smiles a secret smile as her sister unzips a large purse. 'How much do we owe you for the medicine? You must let us pay for that.'

'No, definitely not,' insists Kaisa. 'It's the least I can do.'

Maeve closes the purse and, with her companions, moves to the other side of the room. 'We were wondering how old he is. With his white hair and birthmark...'

'Early thirties, I think,' – the nurse, still writing, 'thirty-one... two...'

'Can he read and write?' continues Maeve, her voice dropping. 'We heard he was a bit...'

'If you mean 'a bit simple', well he's not,' snaps back Kaisa. 'Of course he can write. And as for reading... What else d'you think he's had in his life all these years?'

Maeve is shaken. 'Sorry Kaisa – it's just gossip – hardly anyone we know has ever set eyes on him, but that doesn't stop the stories. And what with his name. Oh dear...'

The nurse takes her hand. 'It's alright Maeve. No-one could have been kinder to him than you and Stevie. All I know for sure is that he spent his childhood up at the Manse, and that so-called nurse had something to do with looking after him'

'Horrible,' whispers Maeve, twisting, untwisting her apron. 'You used to see her with the Dean, didn't you, dear.'

'...horrible...' echoes her sister.

Kaisa shuts her case and walks out under a low arch into the kitchen. At the sink she washes her hands in sweet-smelling soap and dries them on a clean towel. Pans, ladles and serving spoons gleam neatly on the scrubbed walls. Illustrated plates are disposed ship-shapely on the dustless shelves of an oak dresser. So much meticulous congruity. She smiles and hankers after the mild chaos of her own small den.

From a picture-rail hangs a history in grey photographs of two ancient serious little girls with their ma and pa. On either side of the arch hang vases of dried campion and love-lies-bleeding. And framed by the arch are the sisters themselves, matt-glazed figurines in violet and hyacinth. As she moves towards them, into the parlour, the street door swings open. A tall shape enters and melts into the shadow of an antique grandfather clock.

'Best keep your doors and your hearts locked, ladies, in these dangerous days.' Charles de Vere Bottomley-Turrentine, in burlesque mode, whirligigs to centre stage, sweeps a dimpled fedora from his head and bows low with exaggerated courtly grace in response to a burst of delighted giggling from the aunts.
'To what,' enquires the nurse, 'do we owe this unexpected intrusion?' The performance continues. 'To the presence of your beauteous self, most gracious lady. I metaphorically prostrate myself in obeisance before your noble, most... Hello, what's this?' – catching sight of a woolly white head rolling from side to side on the antimacassared sofa. She frowns, raises finger to lips. Three abbreviated snores break the silence. 'What's he doing here?' asks Brownie.
'Kinch Wilkins brought him,' replies Kaisa. 'They arrived this morning in a dreadful state. Pigeon's arm was mangled by one of the Dean's dogs. Neither wanted to talk about it. The boy's asleep upstairs. We thought we'd leave them awhile before bothering them with questions.'

He casts a hard look at the pale wisps covering Pigeon's scalp, and adjusts a greasy frond of his own hair. 'I'm here to pick your brains, Kaisa my love.' Seen close up, the acne on Brownie's cheeks does not convince – colour and texture look authentic but the edges of the latex patch show as a raised contour on the bridge of his nose. 'Might you, my precious, have come across in your travels any associates of one Prudence 'Primrose' Jenkins, defunct, a blind street musician of the *accordéaniste* persuasion?' He glances across at the sisters, who are standing over Pigeon, discussing him in grave undertones. Stevie looks up, catches the newcomer's eye, and asks him if he'd like a cup of tea, mouthing the words.

'Yes, please,' he mouths back at her.

'There is somebody,' says Kaisa. 'An elderly negro woman who lives, or lived, in Paradise Valley. I don't know if there's a connection but on her walls there's an old photo of Primrose Jenkins in all her finery playing concertina on the Cathedral steps. There's a young woman below her, on a lower step, sitting at her feet. It stuck in my memory because it's the only picture of Primrose I've ever seen and it was nothing like that statue in Cathedral Square. People talk like she's a saint but saintliness wasn't the quality that sprang to mind when I saw that picture. But then again the camera can lie, and blind people can look a little grim when they're not talking... still... something about her...'

'Whereabouts in the Valley does she live, this woman?'

'It's some years now – she may not even be alive. Bess, I think, was her name. Never knew her surname. In St. Ebb's Road.'

Stevie appears beside them, delivers a consignment of weak tea, and asks whether Kaisa would like one of the same. Her offer declined, the old lady limps away to the far corner of the room, and opens a door onto a flight of narrow stairs, which she ascends in evident discomfort, one hand on the rail and the other gripping her hip. Brownie and the nurse watch in silence as the slippered feet shuffle upwards out of sight.

'She's gone to look in on Kinch. They've always doted on him,' whispers Kaisa. 'I remember in the old days when his mum was in and out of hospital with his baby sister – he can't have been more than four when it all started. For a couple of years Kinch more or less lived in this cottage. Happiest time of their lives it was – for Maeve and Stevie, I mean.'
'A sister?'
'Dead. Two years of pain and narcosis until pneumonia put an end to it. She never saw the outside of a hospital. Suffer the little children, by Christ...' She looks away.

A larger-and-louder-than-average bluebottle appears from nowhere, crashes into the window, and drops KO'd to the carpet.

The ceiling above them creaks. She continues.
'His poor mum never got over it, coming on top of her husband's disappearance. In a coma for six weeks she was, after the baby died.'

The bluebottle lies on its back in the hub of an aztec sunwheel, waves its legs at them, executes a short buzz to flip itself onto its feet, and lifts off, accelerating in a straight line,
hard again,
at the window...

'She's a lot better now of course, with a job and all, though she still gets the odd spell of vagueness – not so bad she can't cope, just sort of distracted. I haven't seen her for six months but the last I heard she was working part-time at Gridmore's.'

'What's she look like?' asks Brownie. 'I may have come across her.'
'Small and dark. No taller than Kinch. Angry black eyes. One leg wasted from childhood polio, so she walks lopsided, but quick all the same. Doesn't say much.'

A snort from Pigeon draws their attention across the room. Stevie has returned and joined her sister in the kitchen to help with the washing up. Maeve sees Brownie looking at them over the rim of his cup. Eyes twinkling through spangle-framed bifocals, she flashes him a sisterly grin. He swallows a tepid mouthful and carries his cup and saucer over to the sink. 'Thanks, that was lovely.'

Glances at the man on the sofa.
Takes leave of the sisters.

Kisses nurse on cheek. And,
with a flourish of dimpled fedora,

dematerialises.

tab: 22

in which Brownie partakes of a nice lunch

The passage.
Out of.
Emerges from.

Squall of cold
hammers into midriff.
Coatcollar whips
across face,
snicks an eyeball.

'Wheeeeeeee' shrills he,
snatching at the brim of his fancy headgear. Just in time.
Back in the passage he buttons up his trenchcoat, slips the fedora
between his knees, sweeps his hair back with both hands and pulls it
through a loop of cotton-covered elastic into a rogue's ponytail. From an
inside pocket he produces a pair of blue-tinted double-o John Lennon
specs. A modest transfiguration.

Sun gone, hugger-muggered in grey nimbus.

They come.
The market-day faces, the bodies.
The weatherblown clothed bodies caught out shopping.
And food. Whole families of hamburgers, fat anoraked torsos polysected
by orange cheese and pickled cucumber and bright green lettuce.

Chillies on skateboards. Rotting elderly aubergines with cynic leers, weighed down, teeth gritted against the gale, supermarket plastic cutting into fingers. Forkfuls of badly mashed potato clutch their outer garments close against the cold. A choux bun waddles into the King's Head. Shiny black-suited olives queue up in lunchtime sandwich bars alongside upturned artichokes and iced end-of-everything doughnuts.

Lunchtime.

Stomach grabbing at phantoms.

Broken flagstones seesawing underfoot.

Blizzards of human fruit scudding by.

He squints, at, through, between, around,

curved shopglass and flat shopglass, ply on ply.

Hops in a doorway. Hops out.

Cantankers past Butcher the Butcher's,

Loomis Lectrics, W.H. Smith and the Axton Job Centre.

Ricochets off a concrete-filled donkey jacket down a narrow side street, and discovers himself at the chrome and crystal counter of Ed the Ted's Diner, ordering two rounds of hot salt beef on brown with no mustard and a glass of Guinness.

'Will that be all, Mr. T.?'

'That'll be all, Morry... thanks.'

The door bursts open and a clutch of five children spills in, windfelled all over the floor, followed by an ill-wrapt roundhouse of a mother reversing up the single step of the cafe with a baby-filled buggy.

He leaps down from his barstool. Holds open the door.

'Thanks ever so, love. Bwrrrr! Terr'ble innit.'

'Absolutely awful.'

'Darren, see what the others want. Drinks only mind.'

91

Brownie's pile of steaming beef and bread has arrived. He falls upon the meal as ravening hyena, semi-feral chimpanzee, primordial strain of mouthcorner-napkin-dabbing erectable hominoid. Pushes the empty plate aside. Draws to him the dark balm of the Guinness.

Questions... Questions...
This under-the-bath world he's got himself sucked into...
The Dean's unmistakable presence... everywhere...
What real hold does he and his Church have over the city?
And wealth... what wealth?
The Cathedral is solvent but only just, and as for his stipend...
As for the Guild's 30% slice of York National...
As for Gridmores... still taking people on, despite... might be worth...
And where does Clarissa fit in? The 'Nurse' thing's a joke, but is she more than bodyguard, batman and mistress to the devious prelate?
And now the floriated pauper-queen herself...
And Pigeon... Pigeon... Pigeon... ?

Yet again –
storyboarded on a shot nerve –
the interview with the Dean,
eighteen months ago – yet again.
Eighteen months ago, three years
after his arrival with SkuM... his arrival...

Images. Back and forth.
SkuM. A gaggle. A tight collective of systemically unemployed actor/writers cobbled together to bring hard left cabaret to the disaffiliated yeomanry of subtopia. Weeks of wretched ill-rehearsed gigs on the

streets of Farmtown, and the whole shambolic enterprise rounded off
with a vile pubcrawl... double scotch-and-vitriol all round, courtesy of
the Guild... and his rejection by the others in The Mitre, where he stayed
on... and on... In his head nothing remains of the hours between his first
double scotch and the next afternoon, waking up cold and sick under a
park bench in the pelting rain. All those months on the road, just when
things were starting to look up, before Axton that is... even the notices...
The hurt brings on nausea, still.

And then,
the rain-sodden lurch back to the house to find the whole crew
skedaddled, sans trace, not even a scribbled note. Except... in their hurry
they'd overlooked a trunkful of props and make-up, the germen of his
present collection. Had they left it behind on purpose? Anyway, he'd
kept on the flat, which was filthy but cheap, and somehow managed to
get by on busking – plus the odd stint of nightwork, washing dishes in
the Old Town restaurants.

Should've got out there and then, but he'd delayed, was on the point of
leaving, when friends told him they'd seen Terry Colvyn, *de facto* troupe-
leader, unmistakable with that star tattoo under his left eye, hanging
around the open market, second Saturday after the bust-up, waiting for
the stallholders to finish, crawling about with the alkies and bagladies,
scavenging fruit and veg from the gutters.
He'd searched for him the next day,
next days, weeks, but nothing.

And then, the Dean.
The interview, yet again, yet again:

'... *hope my people didn't wake you too early, Mr. Turrentine.*
All this unremunerative kitchen drudgery till the early hours must be,
well, suffocating for a man of your intellectual so-on-and-so-forth, which
is one reason, among several, why we took the liberty of thinking you
might appreciate a change to something rather more... etcetera, etcetera...
... skills of your true...
... work of a sub rosa...
... etcetera...
... true vocation...
... etcetera, etcetera...

'*So.*
The job.
You may well be aware that our Church's high regard for the values of
custom and heritage, although cherished by the overwhelming if silent
majority of our citizens, is in some quarters a source of bitter resentment.
I refer in particular to a small cell of local anarchists. Their ultimate goals
are the usual ones no doubt, but in the short term their priorities seem to
be the undermining of clerical authority and the sabotage of Church-run
businesses. For fifteen years they've been a mildly irritating thorn in our
side but latterly their operations have become more sophisticated. Which is
why the Abbey Guild decided to root them out completely before any real
harm is done. In the early days we had some success. Indeed, we found and
neutralised one of the group. Caught in the act. An amateurish bungler
who tried to start a fire in our furniture factory without even checking on
the night watchman. But he wouldn't talk.
And since then... Nothing.

'Let me give you an idea of their current style.

As you may know, the Cathedral runs a small publishing company, *True Cross Books* – mainly reprints of Christian classics – *Pilgrim's Progress, Historica Ecclesiastica*, that sort of thing. Traditional but non-sectarian. Well, recently a project close to my own heart came to fruition. After 56 years of meticulous toil, one of our own priests, Father Justinian, completed a new translation of the Bible based on a seventh-century Roman text used by followers of the Emperor Constantine, or Saint Constantine as we prefer to call him. *The Milvian Bible* – you may have heard of it. The finished text was electronically transferred from Father Justinian's typescript onto the company's internal network. At some point between proof reading and publication the network was hacked into and a sizeable chunk of Nehemiah Chapter Three removed and supplanted by two pages of revoltingly blasphemous pornography which we now know to have been taken from a piece of filth entitled '*The Amorous Adventures of a Country Priest*'. Thankyou Mr Turrentine... So glad you find it amusing. The error was eventually discovered, but not until three months after publication. However, as luck would have it, the distributors were in a financial mess at the time, and consequently the book had only been delivered to shops in Axton and Farmtown. Unsold copies were recalled immediately, and, thanks to some frantic detective work by my curates, all the others were traced and the owners presented with a new *Milvian Bible*, in its fully checked second edition.

'And there you have it, Mr. Turrentine, the Hand of Divine Providence – shepherding us through the whole nasty business, ensuring the fault was found not by a member of the public but by one of my most trusted senior priests. All in all, the episode was no more than a minor hiccup, but for a Christian publishing house with an international reputation the effects could have been disastrous. *The Bibles might well have been distributed world-wide and thousands sold before anything was noticed. Who, after all, reads Nehemiah? So you see what we're up against. The incidents are infrequent, but they're getting harder to deal with. Thus the Guild's decision to act. Which is where you come in. Your job will be to mingle, observe, and report back, in return for which you will receive a monthly retainer with expenses, plus a generous bonus for every scrap of useful information. You may wonder why we came to you. Well, to be frank I don't like you or your politics, but credit where credit's due, you're no thug and you're not entirely without scruple. We know for instance that when the Trotskyite bunch with whom you were recently associated couldn't make you toe their political line they dumped you, spiking your drink and stealing your money. You didn't know about the drink? There's little escapes the eagle eye of The Mitre's proprietor. One of our deacons. Excellent chap. In short, Mr. Turrentine, you're poor but you're not stupid. You're a professional dissembler with nothing to lose and much to gain.'*

The ledge. The hard blue tarmac.
Something telling him to jump...
Nudging him forward...

'You will deliver a written report, itemising expenses, to my assistant, Nurse Clarissa Mockhardt, at the Silver Spoon Cafe on the first Tuesday of every month. You will be incognito. She will give you money and instructions in a sealed envelope. We don't expect immediate results, but we do expect diligence and discretion. If you change your mind let us know within the next three days. Goodbye, Mr. Turrentine. We won't meet again. Pleasure to do business with you.'

The murmurous babble of children on their best behaviour draws him back to the present. He stands up. The fat woman is chatting to Morry, who sees his nod and shuffles over. From a corner of his wallet Brownie pulls a crumpled note, pays Morry, and turns smilingly toward the noise.

The children are seated at a round table. Darren, a lanky adolescent and clearly something of a hero to his young siblings, is describing in affectionate detail the brain-transplant scene from 'The Curse of Frankenstein', a cod-horror cornerstone of Brownie's own celluloid youth... the gurgle eupeptic of tube/flask/funnel... the squeal euphoric of bonesaw slicing through cranium...

'Happy days, Mr. T,' sighs Morry.
'Happy days, Morry? Yes indeed. Tell me – whatever happened to Ed?'
'Ed? Oh Ed. Ed's long gone. Several owners since him, but we've all kept his name. Thanks very much, Mr. T.'

Brownie pockets his change, trades grins with the children's mother and manages to prevent his gaze from dropping down to the creamy glimmer of what he suspects is a whole naked breast giving nourishment to the youngest member of the family.
'Cheerio Morry,' says he.

And plunges out
once more,
into the tempest.
Turns right.
Away from the High Street.
Past boarded-up conveniences,

past junk shops and charity shops, past down-at-heel estate agents, and then out of the shopping area, through the ramshackle store-yards of Greenland Timber. Wind crashes into him.
Rags of torn polythene blow against his feet,
cling on to him like the orphans of a doomed race.

The pavement gets worse.
He stumbles into grit-filled pot-holes,
trips on erupted flagstones.

At his shoulder, panels of twisted iron slam against their wooden posts. Screeches pierce the wind's roar. Friction. Rusty corrugated metal, rubbing itself against the knuckle of a leafless privet. A huge gust sends the jagged panel swiping out across the footpath,
forcing him into the gutter.
A few more yards.
Stop.

His eyes close for respite against wind and the flying grit.
He re-opens one to regain balance.
A large raindrop shatters itself on the exposed pupil,
drenches his whole being in cold and wetness.
Blinks.
Shakes head.
Raises hands as
awning to brow.

Squints through
wind, grit.

Road drops
away
beneath him.

Wo-ah!

On the brink.

Below,

in a dished glen,
                    postulated by some
as the site of a prehistoric meteorite collision,

skulk the derelict cottages of Paradise Valley.

tab: 23

in which are found an old photograph and a new ally

'Are you Bess?'

Face behind the glass.
Black. Toothless. Malevolent.
'Who's askin'?'

Brownie puts his mouth to a gap between window and frame.
'I'm a reporter from the Gazette. We're doing a feature on Axton in the old days. The district nurse said she'd seen a photo of Primrose Jenkins hanging on your wall and I was hoping you might let me see it and maybe have a few words with you about your life. I can offer you twenty pounds for your trouble.'
The face disappears.
A door opens.
Through the opening
a hand emerges,
curls a pallid forefinger.

Inside.
Through a damp passage, caked with mould.
And into a tiny parlour which to his surprise is neat and well kept and seems clean despite the gloom and airlessness. The woman sits in a white-painted rattan armchair surrounded by cushions. Her head, grinning and only mock-malevolent, looks out over the body of an enormous 12-string guitar.

'Siddown...'
The voice is husky, barely audible.
He sits down on a wooden chair. Drags it closer.
'Name's Bess McVey, outa Birminam Alabama,' she murmers. 'N'ah play
the blues, jes the blues... straight n'natchel.' She lays the 12-string on
the floor and lifts a purple Gibson from a stand beside her.
Fingers crawl over frets.
Hooked tortoiseshell
pulls on braided steel...
plucks... peels...
A cyclone comes,
holds... stops...

She replaces the Gibson, takes up the 12-string.
Starts strong and pure. Son House's 'Death Letter'.
And sings. Entering low in a rough warble,
she hoists the melody two octaves higher.
The tempo increases, hypnotically.
Notes careen in swoops and stalls.
The room tips. Fug turns to honey.
She finishes in the middle register,
flattens her vibrato to beaten gold,
fades finally all away to a rhythmic,
whispered, death-rattle.

He sits trembling,
his flayed white heart
in his hands.

The singer lays down her guitar, pushes herself up from the chair, and leaves the room. She returns a minute later carrying a glass of something inch-thick and tawny. He takes the drink and starts to apologise. She puts a dry hand over his mouth and will hear nothing of it. But he tells her the truth, that he's no journalist, that he's doing the investigating on his own account. 'Well, well, enn *thet* a shame,' she chuckles. 'Don worry boy, anytime you wanna hear ol Bess, you jes c'mon roun, unnerstan. Now. Into my kitchen. I'll show you this picture.'

The photograph is just as Kaisa described.

The two women are seated on the lower steps of the Cathedral, the carved doors of which appear under the bevelled edge of the cardboard mount. Beneath her crown of primroses the old beggar-lady stares at the camera blank-eyed and belligerent. Though evidently now in the last years of her reign, the box of her jaw is still firm. Right hand and concertina are blurred. A stole of mottled fur hangs about her shoulders, partially covering what appears to be a breastful of flashing costume jewellery. The head is slightly turned to show a nose of some delicacy and a tiny twisted slash of mouth. The younger woman sits two steps below and in front, head level with her employer's knee. She is plainly dressed. Her dark hair is pulled straight back from the face and held in place by a narrow band. The look she directs at the camera is empty of feeling. Brownie puts her age at twenty-eight to thirty, finds himself touched by the downturned outer corner of each eye, the pointy chin, the bottom lip sucked in between her teeth. Lizzie, the guide – soon to be cartwheeled into oblivion by a dreaming motorist.

'Nurse you talk about, boy. Mmm... kinda small would that be? Straight-talkin reg'lar tiger-lady?'

'That's her,' laughs Brownie.

'Well now... well... guess you alright, if it really was that fine gal.'

'Kaisa Strachan.'

'Thet's it! Nurse Kaisa. Ten year 'go. Had this foot, see... Big like'n apple, n'so painful I c'n walk at all. In real trouble I was, unnerstan... This town was real good t'ol Bess arter my man left... sure seem strange now... Gimme me that operation on m'ol foot, then look arter me til it heal... that was Nurse Kaisa. Gimme this place rent-free they did. Neighbour-free too now it is, but not then, see. An a small pension... jes enough to eat on. That'n some cleanin's kep me alive... I guess.'

'But your music...?'

'Music's jes for me now,' she rasps, 'since my man gone. Bagfulla slimy bucks, s'all I ever was to him. Hard... still hard... you what?'

He chokes back a further question. 'Nothing... sorry. Turrentine's the name by the way – sometime actor, sometime musician, sometime private investigator, sometime kitchen porter. At your service. Please call me Brownie.'

'Pleased t'make your 'quaintance, Brownie Turrentine. Good t'meet wi'someone who 'preciates the music arter all these years.'

'Pleasure's all mine, Bess, believe me.

Now...

about this picture......'

tab: 24

in which a predator goes about her business

5.00 p.m.
The wind has dropped.

On the Valley pavements
leopard-spots of rain startle the dust.

The blue and green hands on a self-winding waterproof-to-300-metres
ruby-bezelled platinum Rolex jerk around their gold centre-boss. On
the domed glass a red-nailed thumb wipes away each puddle of water as
soon as it appears.

Five minutes, the harbinger shower endures and threatens.
The olive duffel hood slowly twists and slowly twists back.
Over to the east, far away – the stormcloud's heart.
Over Axton – the patchy mist that has been loitering there all afternoon.
The rain stops. A hand slips into a pocket.
Thunder rumbles. Far away.

Opposite,
from inside the desolate terrace,
the howl of a kennelled guitar.

The hand in the pocket
squeezes on the stock
of a short vegetable knife.

Half an hour passes.
A door swings open.
Brownie Turrentine emerges, looks briefly around
before striding off westward down the ruined street.
Skips over a low wall, cuts through an overgrown park,
and climbs the steep road back to the city centre,
his pale coat fanning out in the breeze.
A moth. Crawling up a curtain.

... tck-tck...
... tck-tck...
... tck-tck...
... tck-tock...

Olive duffel coat
crosses street,
inserts a key
into a lock,

opens a door,
stalks along a
mould-blackened passage.

tab: 25

"possible enemy ship sighted, bearing red nine-zero degrees!...
all units to action stations... prepare to dive!"

commander kinch wilkins, master of his majesty's submarine *seek-the-foe*, feels his knees pricked and pocked by the tassels fringing the oceanic blue of the front room carpet. his right knee particularly is hurting, where the wool has worried itself into a cluster of knots. leaning sideways, he lifts his leg to reposition it in a gap between the tassels, on a cool varnished floorboard.

the hull of the submarine has been crudely fashioned from a ten-inch block of white deal. its only embellishment is the conning-tower, and even this, in truth, resembles nothing more nautical than an empty cotton reel with the rims chewed off. the forrard deck is split by a deep groove running from prow to conning-tower. this is the torpedo gulley, along which the steel-tipped torpedoes are launched, crossbow-style, by a ribbon of thick elastic.

firing the 'tinfish' is a hazardous business. with the elastic hooked over a notch cut into its shaft, the torpedo is pulled back along the groove until another notch at its rear engages with a click into the base of the conning-tower. from the centre of the tower rises a thin dowel, the periscope, which also serves as firing-pin. when this is pushed down, the torpedo leaps from its mooring and shoots along the floor. the procedure requires great delicacy as the slightest knock can cause the missile to fire prematurely. one broken window and numerous round dents in walls and furniture have led his mother to insist on pain of confiscation that all loading be carried out on the floor.

on the opposite side of the three-yard ocean, anchored among swirling bays of amber and terre verte, floats the cruiser *tintagel*, built of close-fitting separate wooden bricks, each lacquered with its own tint of grey. in the hull's mid-section, at water-level, is a narrow brick which bears the ship's name. this is the visible edge of a mousetrap-like spring detonator which, when hit by a torpedo, hurls the dozen blocks high into the air, scattering them to the far corners of the room.

splat-splat-splat.
waves against the port flank.
flecks of spray, sown into the breeze,
salting his lips, dribbling down the lens of his spectacles.

"all units to action stations," repeats the commander, "prepare to dive." he clambers down the fixed vertical ladder, closing the conning- tower hatch over his head, glad to hear the orderly bustle of his men as they settle into their diving stations. throb-throb. throb-throb. throb of the engines. throb of his heart. blinking, eyes adapting to the gloom, he pulls off his glasses to polish the lens on the hem of his t-shirt.

"ready to dive, commander," announces a steady voice at his side.
"periscope depth, lieutenant. prepare to fire torpedoes from all tubes. third hand's aft. I'll go forrard."
"ay, ay, sir."

the first lieutenant removes his cap, runs a hand over his frizzy white crew-cut and puts his lips to the funnel of a brass speaking-tube. "lieutenant cleary to engine room. dive to periscope depth and hold at five knots." "ay, ay, sir," comes the reply.
"bridge to helmsman," continues the lieutenant, "set course for the enemy cruiser on starboard bow."
"ay, ay, sir."

five minutes later commander wilkins arrives in the fore torpedo cabin and watches from the doorway as gunner's mate petty officer abel matthews, clad in nothing but a peaked cap and greasy loincloth, single-handedly lifts a one-and-a-half ton torpedo into the starboard firing tube. on its nosecone is scrawled in black and crimson the caricature of a murderous dog. the gunner's mate stretches out a fingertip to stroke the back of the dog's neck before closing off the tube. he turns toward his captain and as he does so the grin on his face dissolves and coalesces into the blood-caked jaws of a steel mantrap. "ready and standing by, commander," clanks the spectre, fat hand to temple.

the commander returns the salute and drags his gaze sideways to the second torpedo tube, manned by the taller but frailer shape of petty officer james creech, whose limbs are sticks of jaundiced bamboo and whose head is still curing into its final imago, that of a giant squirrel-plucked fir cone. not knowing how to address this eyeless mouthless creature and seeing that its tube has already been loaded, he salutes, slams shut the cabin door, and strides back to the bridge.

the sound of water sluicing around the submarine's ballast pipes announces the start of the shallow dive. "up periscope!" he barks, seizing the tube by its handles, crouching down to peer through the rising visor. the scope's upper window breaks out of the waves into the sunshine. nothing. nothing but the even belly of the horizon. he swivels it round. has he been mistaken?
no. there it is. a dark squat mitre, more rock than ship.
"target vessel closing at twelve knots, sir," says the radiologist.

"fire torpedo one."
the submarine shudders.
dishes rattle in the galley.
"fire torpedo two."

one minute passes.
he can just about discern
the merged wakes of the two torpedoes.
four minutes.

he calculates it will take another minute for the torps to reach their prey. the periscope handles are slimy with sweat. the visor cuts into the bridge of his nose. seawater trickles down the instrument's column onto his head. as he watches, the cruiser swings slowly round to present the whole length of her hull as target.

"broadside on," he grins.

* * *

inside his berth,
aboard the modified 'southampton' class cruiser *hms tintagel*,
captain kinch wilkins dso rn is taking a nap.
the flying dream.
again...

*in a driven surge of will, he levitates from the pavement, rising slowly
above the heads of a growing audience of reverential familiars and
flabbergasted strangers. as he rises, the strain eases. arms wingwide,
body horizontal, he glides forward, borne along on updraughts of his
own exhilaration, high over a busy shopping mall. the area resembles
ship street. the architecture is much the same but the road is wider
and lined with the canvas-roofed stalls of farmtown market. shoppers
look up in disbelief. they wave and shout but he doesn't respond. he
swoops low to impress a gang of boys crowded round a toyshop window.
they see his reflection in the glass and turn to look up, on cue,
astonished – all that is except one, the smallest, who bends gutterwards,
curling his fingers around a lump of red brick.
he angles his feet, soars up again,
out of harm's way. levels.
steadies himself.
banks left,
over martyrs memorial, home to an infamous act of reformation butchery,
but better known these days as a magnet for axton's ragbag fraternity of
bohos and dropouts. he circles, looking for friendly faces. just a few. on
the stone benches. talking. not looking up at him.
power deserts him. he falters.
pitches. yaws.
head dips,*

and down he plummets, down, down,
spun and spreadeagled into the imploding city.
again...

and then awakes.
to echoes, and crashes,
and the world turning over.
"bridge to captain! bridge to captain! come in please."
"captain to bridge. what the hell's going on?"
"lieutenant creech speaking, sir. we're hit amidships port side. small
to medium mine or non-contact torpedo."
the captain watches his hands shaking,
fumbling with his bootlaces -
"are damage control parties on the way?"
"yes, sir. they'll be there by now. we've a two degree list to port."
"slow to ten knots, lieutenant, and commence zigzagging. i'll be
with you directly."
"ay ay, sir."

in a benighted crew messroom, lower deck forrard, the air is thick with
smoke and yelling. the feeble glow from two isolated bonfires of
bedding and laundry is soon augmented by a dozen blades of yellow
torchlight. one of the torches finds a rating, trapped under a steel girder,
on his back, arm broken at the elbow and twisted under his body.
the voice of petty officer kaisa strachan is heard, muffled by her
breathing mask. "watch out, there's wounded here – get the first aid
party – tell them to come down with stretchers. quick, dosser, get an
extinguisher on that fire, damn you!"

"ay ay, p.o. – i'm on it."

"damage control h.q., this is midship repair party reporting from messroom three juliet port. we're taking in water through a medium-sized hole and several pepperholes. small fires in crew mess tiger five, and a localised power failure. specialist parties are dealing with all damage. over and out."

she glances round. "scotty, stop dreaming! over here and use the splinter box to plug that leak!" – screeching in an effort to be heard over the din of male shouting and the crackle of fire and the slushing to and fro of an ankle-deep stew of lumpy seawater. "help me jam it in place with the shores. you two, stop the pepperholes with bungs and wedges. oh shit..!" the skin of her right shoulder catches on a jag of exploded bulkhead. "tonks, you and nodger come off the fire and help b-group plug that hole with the mattress and mess table. and wipe that smirk off your face or you'll be spending a week in the cells!"

"emergency lines up and running, p.o.," yells a voice behind her as she is suddenly blinded by the brilliance from a string of lightbulbs hung close above her head. she blinks and blinks again.

"petty officer strachan reporting to damage control h.q. – fires in mess room under control, bulkhead leaks plugged, and electrical power partially restored by emergency cables. two stretcher cases removed to sick bay. will examine for further damage. over and out."

* * *

inside the sub, disappointment spreads from commander to crew. what had first appeared to be a spectacular bullseye is now shown to have caused no more than minor embarrassment to the large cruiser. one hit with a defective warhead, and one complete miss.

with his face pressed to the periscope, the commander waits for the counter-attack. but he sees no torpedo boats emerge from behind the grey bulk of the enemy ship and no reconnaissance planes launched from her deck. whilst maintaining her general northwesterly course, the cruiser has started precautionary zigzagging and slowed to ten knots. but no retaliation.

he waits. still nothing. perhaps her asdic is down.
he can't believe his luck. the weather too, is perfect. a fresh wind makes the white horses leap in the bright sunshine, giving perfect cover to the plume of spray thrown up by the periscope.
"all crew to action stations. prepare to fire torpedoes three and four."

* * *

aboard the *tintagel*, the captain clanks down the metal rungs connecting the ship's laundry to the forrard steering position, on his way to inspect the damage in three juliet port.

he allows himself a nod of satisfaction. a few timely decisions have corrected the two degree list to port without any change to the speed or zigzag course of his cruiser. he feels sure they've hit a stray mine, but has ordered the zigzagging to continue, just in case it's a maverick enemy sub, unaware that the war is over. just in case.

the toe of his shoe has found the next rung and is just taking the weight of his body when the second torpedo strikes. the ship quakes. jerks him off the ladder. into free fall. his descent follows in parallel the path of the ladder. an uninterrupted vertical. and down he falls, through two deck-hatches, missing the steel frames and crashing onto the floor of the common machine shop, which is where he finds himself on regaining consciousness a moment later.

riots rage in his head. a jacket of opaque gum has attached itself to his eyeballs. hurting all over, he manages to get to his feet, only to lose control of balance and direction. now he is sliding, propelled forward over the slippery floor. he blinks his eyes to clear away the sticky fog and feels himself stumbling through a raised doorway, bundled and rolled across an iron mesh platform, off the edge, into free fall again. thump... his back... thump... shoulder... – pingponged back and forth between the lagged steampipes which snake through the wellspace of the forrard boiler room – down and down again. the impact of his bare head on the waffled floor is preceded by a loud explosion. the loudest. the third torpedo. and then nothing.

he is woken by someone scrambling over him. a heavy boot stomps on his balls. the pain hardly registers – just the heat, and the bestial clamour of whinnies and squeals and hissing steam. he is sitting wedged against one of the four giant boilers, pouring sweat. he reaches up, grabs the wheel of a huge gate-valve, and pulls himself to his feet. billows of white steam cut visibility to arm's length. for some reason he finds himself reciting by heart the boiler tube leak drill, turning the gate-valve to shut off the oil supply to the sprayers – "...secure all tubes or doors on the boiler. two, increase speed of fans" – cranking up the lever to maximum – "three, open safety valves on damaged boiler" – his fingers slithering in vain over the greasy taps.

a powerful hand covers his. he turns to confront a boiler-suited rating with a face swollen on one side into a long purple blister. "come with me, sir. they're closing the air-locks." the seaman drags him away from the boiler and together they struggle on through the hot mist. something has happened to his sense of balance. he realises that his ship must be listing to starboard by about twenty degrees.

they climb higher. the heat becomes unbearable. the coiled pipes of the cavernous boiler room are gargantuan maggots inflated by fever, ready to burst boiling venom all over him and his helper. the iron steps and gangways are melting the soles of his shoes. whenever he grips a rail to pull himself up, the skin of his hands sizzles so that by the time they reach the air-lock exit it is hanging off his fingers in black ribbons. they pass the bodies of at least seven men, alive but burnt beyond help. they hear the cries of many more.
how many of his 800 crew are left?
is this the end?

the second lieutenant and some lower ratings are waiting to pull him and his companion through the airlock. as soon as they're through, the doors are slammed shut and bolted, condemning the rest of the poor bastards down there to a hellish death.

he leans back against a sloping bulkhead, shoulder to shoulder with the rating who has saved his life, whom he now recognises, despite the monstrous blister, as able seaman pigeon cleary. they struggle to catch their breath. pigeon squints up at an overhead sign. the ship's bakery. "thankyou...." begins the captain, which is as far he gets. following a paff-paff of distant explosions, the cruiser gives a lurch and tilts another few degrees. they fall into the open doorway of the bakery and slide on their rumps across the floor through a puddle of grey sludge. down and down and into a buffer of rough cushions. cool... firm... grainy... sacks... sacks of white flour...
smelling of vanilla and hazelnut.

the air too is cooler. a breeze. a porthole, open. overwhelmed by a lust for sleep, he closes his eyes to shut out forever the lunatic day. pigeon shakes him by the arm. yells in his ear. "the operations room, sir – we have to see if they've put out an s.o.s. come on sir. it's not far."

the captain wants to sleep. but it is not to be and he feels no anger as he is slapped across the face, yanked to his feet, and dragged up the steep bakery floor back into the passage.

pigeon leading, they fight their way through the scalding smog along the neverending corridor, in the awkward angle between floor and the starboard bulkhead. uphill again. steeper. screams come from everywhere but they see no-one. at every step the ship trembles and lists a little more. the stern is going down. they find a couple of abandoned lifejackets and struggle into them. the smoke thins and the captain sees they are in the common machine shop. the smoke returns. he chokes, and the world spins. pigeon holds him up until the swoon passes, then guides him through a maze of drills, lathes, and vices to a small door on the opposite side of the room. across another corridor and they'll be in the operations room. with his back to his captain, the seaman bends toward the door to check if the way is clear. as his head ducks under the brass lintel, there is another explosion. a ball of orange flame roars down the corridor, transforming his silhouette in the cramped doorway to a lump of black obsidian, haloed in light and fire. there follows a cymbaling of steel on steel, of flying metal debris, of doors, lockers, shelving, pipework, of things torn from their welded moorings, hurtling down the flue of the corridor.

when pigeon draws back from the door
he is headless.
headless.
the half-neck is plugged by a wad of cauterized gristle. but he stands. walks. reaches. he reaches for and holds onto his captain's arm. and leads him through the door, along the fireducted corridor, past the operations room, their destination once but now no more than sputtering heaps of ash and molten alloy. and hauls him up the poker-hot rungs of a diagonal ladder, through a brass-rimmed hatch, and out into bliss itself, the cool evening air of the fo'c'sle deck.

that's better. the captain shakes himself. much better. he has dozed off and woken up alone, on his feet and propped against hot steel with his left arm threaded through a pair of brackets supporting the stairway to the admiral's bridge. someone has bandaged his useless hands into the shape of linen-covered spatulas. pigeon. pigeon. gone now.

he makes his way uphill until he finds himself on the bulkhead of the forrard crew messdeck. he looks around. the situation is bad. his beautiful ship is floating on its side, bow in the air, quarterdeck submerged, main deck cambered to a watery chute.

another lurch. sixty degrees.

the stern sinks lower.

"abandon ship," he yells, roused by duty, vowing to himself he'll be the last to jump ship but won't to leave it so late that he's sucked down into the whirlpool of the final plunge. there are shouts above his head. he looks up in time to see three of his crew leaping off the bofors gun-mounting and dropping toward the sea in a flurry of arms and legs. without life jackets. "o christ, the idiots!" he crawls his way to number one funnel and pulls free a cork-edged floater net. he flings it clear into the sea and then, glancing down through the veins of black smoke, sees with satisfaction several tiny figures clinging to the rope mesh. further out a dozen or so more bodies are bobbing in the swell, only a few with lifejackets. among the bodies with the yellow jackets, he thinks he glimpses one without a head. maybe. maybe not.

what else?

the rafts!

hooking his arms over the rim of the deck, he clambers up onto the port side. here they are, lashed to the deck with thick ropes. but no good. the toggle pins holding the ropes are beyond his reach.

more crashes. an arrow of flame spits from a nearby porthole.

get back.

the deck shimmers with heat as he climbs and scrambles his way back up towards the bow. the ship is listing by eighty degrees. at last he reaches the big 6-inch gun turrets. from the base of 'a' turret he drops onto the 'b' turret bulkhead. above the grinding deathcroak of his ship, he hears a new noise. a jackal baying. and then – "help me lord almighty fucking god – o help me!" – to his left, beyond the capstan. with shoulders pressed back to the smouldering deck he shuffles sideways along the turret, peering through the smoke. there. as he thought. the ship's chaplain, clinging to the u-shaped projection of the starboard fairlead.

though all feeling has gone from his hands and feet, the captain guesses that with a little luck he can still make it to the helpless priest. dropping to his knees, he crawls backwards along the turret casing. his feet search for and find the barrel of one of the 6-inch guns. he opens his legs, wincing as he drops astride the barrel. using his hands for poles, he punts his way toward the nozzle.

another explosion. bowel-deep. he is thrown from the gun onto the griddle of the main deck and is slithering down to his death when the ship judders and rears up suddenly out of the water, leaping forward and coming to rest almost level. his slide is halted by a tangle of tarpaulins and floater nets knotted around the starboard lifelines.

he realises what has happened. the ship has broken in half. whatever occurs now, it's a matter of only minutes before the end.
and then, magically, the smoke clears.

his eyes scan the ocean for survivors. at first, nothing but acres of rolling tar. but then, a new roughness on the surface. misshapen pimples. scabs. a few of the pimples move. some of the scabs break open,

peel, fragment.
some of the fragments scream.
some wave,
their black limbs thrashing air.
nothing he can do.
he looks round. sees the chaplain
still flypapered to the fairlead.

a plan, a memo, to himself: –
crawl across deck... scrabble along the parallel anchor cables... over
brakeslips... over screwslips... past the starboard hawse-pipe, conduit for
the anchorchain... from deck to ship's flank... flank... flank of the ship,
where the great anchor nests, he thinks... thinks... comfortless, like, he
thinks, the breastbone... of a big... primeval... he thinks... big... big...

exhaustion arrives in a tidal rush. arms buckle at the elbow. cheek
slaps hard against the deck. more pain. a sizzling sound and the sweet
biscuit smell of burning flesh. he tries to raise himself. pulls what's left
of his face off the deck. slips a jacketed forearm twixt head and metal.
the half-ship creaks and pitches upward, turning the deck once more
into a cliff of plutonic steel. he spreads his arms, falls a few feet and
finds himself wedged into a gap between the deck-edge and a partially
severed clump cathead.

he looks up.
the chaplain is above him in his long soutane, folded over the
fairlead like a wet sock, legs held by the anchorchain, both broken,
snapped forward at the knee. but alive. still alive.

the head twists around,
and he knows it for what it is,
as ever, desiccated, cadaverous, untouched by doubt.
the skin has roasted from parchment to charred rosebark, but the jaw still
bites the lips to a crushed staple and the eyes still glint like beads of milk
and sapphire. "good afternoon, cap'n wilkins," says the dean.

the creature smiles,
and as he smiles the cheeks split
and two columns of black dust
sift down onto the captain's face.
the creature speaks. "been waiting for you,
your pal and i. but i knew you'd turn up.
always turn up in the end, do you not?
i told him. but would he listen?"

"who?"

"o my dear captain, allow me to introduce
a much-loved associate of yours...
who, i must say, has got rather ahead of himself."

thick smoke drifts between them,
muffling the distant noises to silence.

he can now see his old enemy only through brief gaps in the pall.
sees him reaching behind the fairlead. more smoke.

another gap.

the dean.
facing him.
something heavy in his hands.
a large berry, big as a head.
burned, blistered on one side,
but on the other...
nosed... eyed...
mouthed.
a head,
pigeon's head,
alive,
calling to him.

the hands let go.
the head slips.

pigeon. falling.
dropping past.

oh pigeon.
only a head,
are you?

flying,
are you?

oh pigeon,
pigeon,
...

tab: 26

which tells of certain strange events unfolding on the city walls

8.00 p.m.
The Blood Wall,
north section,
outer parapet.
Rain, easing.

On dimpled blush of wet rock
the rat's toes tap and grip.
The eyes give nothing away.
Brown bobbin. Dun shuttle.
Diagonal. Edge to edge.
Food hard to come by.
Now and then a crumb of soggy biscuit turns up,
or even, prized above all, a lug of meat
trapped in the joints between the marble blocks.

The central gully is awash with rills of dusty water.
Some of the drainage culverts are blocked by buboes of viridian moss
and fine-caulked by the leafmould from last year's buddleias. But some
are clear, and through each of these the rainwater trickles down to the
lip of a zinc spout. Around the unblocked inlets there are no puddles,
allowing the rat an easy passage from outer to inner parapet, where food
is more plentiful. With its prehensile claws the exhausted rodent
clambers nosefirst down the chisel-nicked wall. Alighting on the gully
floor, it shows no interest in scaling the opposite parapet but continues

westward, halting every few seconds, as if for breath. The rain no longer thuds into its sodden back. But the head hangs to the ground.
The teeth chatter.
A cough.
A sneeze.
Move on.

The Wall at this point crosses a low hill and the gully slopes upward, leaving a long stretch clear of standing water. No foodscraps here, but the rat seems content to falter forward, out of the weather.
The rests grow longer. The eyes narrow.
The jaw scuffs ground. The tail drags, stiff.
Forelegs crumple. Unaware.
Unaware of a presence overhead,
ten times the height of any rat,
looming, leering down from the parapet.
The rat limbs spasm. The body rolls sideways.
Pink foam bubbles from the rat mouth.

Above,
a spindly bitch mongrel
checks her rear,
and drops to the gully floor.

Four other dogs arrive.
Preliminary formalities are waived. The rat's carcass is ripped from the mongrel's teeth. A heated debate ensues over the rights of community versus the rights of the transcending individual. The transcending individual, a leaden-eyed male of lupine and Newfoundland ancestry,

holds sway, bolting his prize in the interval between two dog heartbeats. The losers cower, turn, retreat. Satisfied, the victor lopes away from the scene of his triumph, stopping briefly to deposit a steaming pyramidal heap in the centre of the gully.

Dusk.
Unbending.
Into darkness.

A pool of torchlight.
Moving this way.
Between the parapets.

Sluff. Sluff-sluff. Sluff. Sluff-sluff.
The toecaps of two elderly rubber boots dip in and out of the torchlight and come to rest side by side before the hillock of dung. A longhandled shovel descends from the gloom, scoops up the soft heap, and tips it into a lidded leather bucket which has appeared beside the boots.

Boots, bucket and shovel move off again.
Torchbeam swings left-right, left-right. Whenever a turd slips into view, the boots stop, the procedure is repeated. Eventually the light finds a low stone trough filled with water. The boots stop again. Bucket and shovel are laid to ground. The torch is placed on the parapet edge, pointing inwards. The owner of the boots is revealed – a boy of fifteen or sixteen, caped in a dark oilskin, eyes hidden under the peak of a red baseball cap. He rolls a heavy rucksack off his back and onto the parapet, next to the torch. Loosening the drawstring to open the mouth of his rucksack, he lifts out two plastic carrierbags and empties their contents onto a raised

platform near the water trough. From the first, a pungent mess of bones and dried meat. From the second, a clatter of hard biscuits. The empty bags are folded, pocketed. He peels a tight rubber gauntlet from his right hand, inserts four fingers into his mouth and blows out a soaring rocket of a whistle. Within moments of the echoes dying away he senses a low rumble underfoot, a kind of drumming.

A tumult of yelps...

One after another, a rabble of fifteen dogs skids into the hoop of light and sets to devouring the yardlong levee of cookies and dried meat. The youth, who has by now worked his fingers back into the rubber glove, lingers to scratch one of the smaller dogs roughly on the neck. He throws the rucksack over his shoulder, gathers up bucket and shovel, and reaches over the light for the invisible stem of his torch. He then resumes his journey eastward, away from the spoked wheel of canine backs, stopping every so often to deposit of a fresh load of guano into his leather bucket.

tab: 27

in which a youth is accosted by a 'mysterious stranger'

8.30 p.m.
Chillier,
by the minute.

Night daubs its black ire
on the North Axton rooftops,
on the Wall, over the wasted fields.

Between the peaks of Wenlock Ridge
and a bar of low cloud,
the six-day moon clicks up another notch.

To the east of the Ridge stands a solemn convocation of granite tors, the Five Men, under whose scrutiny message-laden ghosts flutter from tree to tree, casting ripples on the ancient battleplain of the Moor. Stubs of bombed-out barn or cowshed can be made out, reminders of a time when the whole area, to within three hundred yards of the Blood Wall, was used as an army firing range.

Beneath the north face of the Wall, tucked into the rebate of the old moat, squat the cubes and domes of Wordsworth Farm, a newfangled military complex known hereabouts as 'The Farm'. The living quarters are underground. From rows of identical square portholes, light is thrown onto the concrete car park in lurid orange slabs. Work pushes on apace, even at this hour.

On the inner side of the Wall, in its ghetto of gothic pseudo-vicarages, a choice filtration of the Old Town exquisites and culturati are sitting-down-to, or staggering-up-from, their evening repast. No more than three dozen in number by their own reckoning, they have modelled this enclave of North Axton into a cosy sanctum sanctorum of the intellect. The patio windows are uncurtained. Through landscaped pine and eucalyptus seeps a fine lemon lustre.

Time passes.
Sky fidgets.
To the north,
behind a palisade of poplars, the Wall is in hiding.
The moon ducks under a fist of cloud. No stars now.
A thin meniscus of sulphuric brilliance teeters eastward, along the Wall, through the inky river which separates the houselights from the lights of The Farm.
Eastward.
Now, it stops.
It. Boy. Torch.
It stops where a barrier of sharp steel spikes cuts across the top of the Wall. The boy downs his torch, pulls a key from his rucksack and opens a gate in the steel fence. On turning to reclaim his torch from the parapet, he sees the steady nucleus of the light start to wobble. It swings round, points its beam into his eyes, and lifts itself to chest height.
And stays there.

The boy staggers back, tripping over his bucket, collapsing bonehard onto the wet marble with his back to the steel spikes.

'What's your name?' enquires a pitiless wheedle. 'Your name, son?'
Silence.
'Name. Your name, damn you!'
'Colin... '
'Where you from, Colin?'
'Can't say...'
'Tut tut... You do this every night?'
'Yessir... twice a night, sir.'
'You what?... You shovel shit twice a night?'
'Nossir... twice to feed... only once to collect droppings... Eight o'clock
and four o'clock... this time of year.'
'Four in the morning?'
'Yessir.'
'Who pays you?'
'Don't get paid sir. Just pocket money. Duty sir. All got duties.'
'Indeed. And the bucket?'
'I leave it at the East Barbican. Don't know after that.'
'And now, Colin... Your benefactor's name. If you please.'
'Sir?'
'Name of employer, Colin. Boss. He who must be obeyed.'
'No sir. No names sir please.'

The glare is only two feet from the boy's face.
He can see nothing of his inquisitor. From beneath the torch a silver-
tipped rod of polished mahogany enters the lightpool and glides
towards him, catching him under the throat and pushing the back of
his neck against the steel posts. 'This is a walking stick, old son,' sneers
the voice. 'But not an ordinary walking stick. If I flick this lever on the
handle with my thumb, a knifeblade will spring out of the cold metal

tip you can feel pressing against your throat. Windpipe first, then
spinal cord. Paralysis or death. Either or both. And now the name...
Please...?'
'Ssssss-chhhclls.'
The pressure eases.
'Try again.'
'Sss-cales.'
'Who?'
'Watford Scales, sir'
The stick goes away.
The boy pulls off his cap,
using it to wipe the sweat from his face.
The torchbeam drops.
'Sorry about that, Colin. No knife, see. I lied. Just a walking stick.
You alright, lad?' The boy nods. 'A couple more questions, then I'll
go. How long have you been doing this?'
'Bout a year. Since Confirmation.'
'Now listen. Try to think. Are you sure you don't know what happens
to the bucket, or what it's for?'
'No idea, sir. I'm a Lay Steward, is what Mr. Scales says. Keeping the
Wall clean and the Church strong.'
'Are there others like yourself?'
'A few, sir. We all collect droppings but I'm the only one who does
the Wall, which is the most important job.'
'What about Scales?'
'Please sir I have to go now.'
'Alright. Take this.'
A banknote is stuffed into the boy's pocket.
The torch descends to the parapet,
still pointing in his direction.

The footsteps retreat.
Silence.

One minute later, fifty yards east,
a trench-coated figure can be seen walking quickly along the inner parapet. When the houselights are close enough, the figure halts, drops to its knees, and crawls backward over the edge, legs dangling in air, elbows taking the weight. Feet kick space till they find the top rung. Then, down the ladder, but slipping, falling to the ground.

'Stupid! Stupid!'
Retrieve military grandpa's heirloom cane.
Return the borrowed ladder to its home
in the lean-to shed of the darkest house.
Jump over patio walls. Scramble over garden fences.
Scuttle down a tree-lined private road.
Through a labyrinth of backlanes.

And, briefly,
out into the lights
of Tiger Street.
And enter,
and finally, enter,
with circumspection,
a brown peeling doorway
between two shops.

tab: 28

in which the 'mysterious stranger' dons a disguise

9 p.m.
In his room. Brownie
throws his coat on the bed,
and stands facing a full-length mirror.
'You crock of shite,' his murky twin snarls back at him.
No lamps have been lit in the cavernous attic room. Outside, he can hear
the sheepish giggles of pranksters from The Bull And Castle a couple of
doors away, trying to hoopla a lamppost with a bike-tyre.
He turns. Rams a fist into his eye.
Grinds the socket.

Think. Think. Think.

He tugs the curtains together.
Stabs a finger at the lightswitch.
Strips, stark shiver-shaky naked.
Slips his skinny weasel body into the shower cubicle.

And emerges ten minutes later. Re-born. Peony-pink and primed for
battle. On goes the monkbald wig from the wig rack, and then a
bulging latex nose. The armature. Around which to construct:-
Persona No. 9, Hackney Jack,
street trader, mid-fifties, puce, patriotic,
one bloodied-but-unbowed assemblage
of self-serving foul-mouthed anglo chirpiness.

tab: 29

which records some alarming discoveries made
in the house of Harold Admetus

10 p.m.
The porch.
Vaulted sandstone.
Dim lantern dangling from the apex.

He doesn't see the bell at first.

A tablet of brushed platinum, upper half striated by the scallopped gills of an art-nouveau entryphone, would like to suggest, not without irony, an incumbent of flamboyant sophistication. Above it glints an oblong of lacquered brass inscribed *Prof. H. Admetus. M.A.(Cantab.)*. Brownie runs his hand over the wall, expecting to find a bellbutton sunk into the brickwork, but then notices, on the lower plate, cut discreetly into the metal, a small circle.

Inside the house, a buzzer buzzes.
'Ye-e-e-e-s,' crackles the intercom.
'A God-fearin Englishman, sir, to see the master of the house.'
'Name?'
'Jack Lyons, guvnor. Ackney Jack they call me. Lyons by name an lion by nature. Raised, felled an raised again in the wog-ridden gutters of our steamin metropolis, with somethin to show you an somethin very private to tell you... for your ears alone... '
No reply.

From the bogus tradesman's neck four leather straps stretch down to the fretted plastic walls of a baker's pallet, packed on both sides with rolled dishcloths and tins of cheap toiletries, and in the middle with felt-lined boxes containing a midget pharmacy of stoppered jars.
He leans back from the door, right foot on the single step,
knee taking the weight of his portable shop.
Muscles twitch, in his neck.

The door is opened by a young oriental woman in a William Morris housecoat. He steps forward. Hands her a business card.
The woman's cheeks are flushed.
At her temples, where the hair seems wet and stuck to the skin, beads of opaque whitish fluid are forming. He stares hypnotized as they trickle down past the ear, onto the sallow neck.
'No visitors please, sir. Professor tired.'
His gaze drops lower. Only three of the buttons are engaged. Through a two inch gap he glimpses the undercurve of a small breast, and beneath it a splinter of white belly.

The door is closing when a dark apparition lours up behind her from the depths of the hall. 'Ok, Han, I'll see to it,' adjures the apparition. The shy girl-woman is supplanted by a monolith of dressing-gowned hoity-toity. Paisleypattern tadpoles squirm up a river of claret.

Brownie knows too well the flapping bewhiskered jowl and autocratic eye. He backs away, out of the light. 'Gr'evenin guvnor. 'Ope you'll forgive this hunwarranted intrusion into the peace of your evenin but I 'ave 'ere numerous inexpensive 'ousehold items of himpeccable quality, as well as a selection of traditional 'erbal remedies made accordin to secret recipes passed on to me by my maternal grandmother, a world-famous 'ealer in 'er own day or so I'm told. If you'd be so kind as to ask a true patriot inside for a small drop of somethin revivin, well then, we could discuss all this... plus p'raps the possibility of a little you-know-what on the QT, if you get my drift.'

Within its purse of skin, the academic eye hardens.
'Something private, you said.'
The pedlar glances round over his shoulder.
'Not 'ere, sir. Streets 'ave ears an eyes an gawd only knows what else. Scuse my french guvnor, but can we go inside?'

The professor motions the visitor over the threshold and leads him through a spacious hall, past a sweep of staircase and into a book-lined study of modest but agreeable proportion. He pulls a tiny liqueur glass and a large bottle of brandy from a cupboard set into the main bookcase. Quarter-fills the glass. Replaces the bottle.
Brownie takes the glass.

Flopping onto an antique davenport, the languid pedagogue hoists one silk-clad knee over its beloved brother. The gown slips apart to disclose a naked column carpeted in grey fur, more cat scratching-post than human leg. 'Now I hope you're not going to waste my time.'
Brownie raises the golden ichor up to an electric candle.
A sniff, a sip, and down in one.
'Nice drop that, guvnor... 'drop' bein the hopprative word.'
With an impatient snort Admetus hauls himself to his feet, snatches back the glass and refills it, this time to the brim.
'Thankyou guvnor. Huncommon generous of you I'm sure. 'Ere's to

135

dear ol Blighty, an a lingerin death to all 'er enemies within an without if you take my meanin no names no pack drill, mum's the word an a nod's as good as a wink between ourselves, an... my lips are sealed until the time is right an ripe... if you take my meanin, guvnor...' Tap-tap-tap. Right index finger. Right nostril.

'The matter, oaf. More matter with less bloody art if you please.'

'Aah, well, sir. I'm a business man first an foremost whose business is movin stock... lightnin my load, so to speak. So what can I interest you in? Solids or...'

'Do you or do you not have some information for me?'

'All in good time, guvnor, but business first. Solids or liquids is it? Medicinal or domestic? Take your time... I'll sit down if I may while you make up your mind,' says Brownie as he berths his tray on a grandiose teak writing desk and makes himself at home in the only available chair, a winged leather buttonback which he drags out from under the desk.

'Tsss.. Alright, damn and blast you... I'll fetch the maid.'

Exit polyhistor, in pout.

On returning with the maid,
Admetus discovers his visitor
sunk, or so it would seem,
into a noisily adenoidal coma.

But.
Not so.
Brownie Turrentine is awake.
Awake, as he has never been.
Head slumped forward, body shaken by tremendous snores, he observes the couple through the tiny sliver of space separating upper from lower

eyelids. They are facing him. He can see most of the maid, but very little of her employer, who is standing close behind her with his head and shoulders out of sight. They remain in the same position for an eternity, the young woman apprehensive, awaiting instructions. The man seems to be murmuring something, very softly, into her ear. She tries to smile. Between the ebb and flow of his own snores, Brownie hears a sound. The sound of ripping cloth.

The maid is distressed.
Something strange is happening to her body.
Her breasts seem to come alive, wriggling like tethered ferrets under the housecoat. Suddenly one of the ferrets breaks free and scuttles down to the groin, where it appears to start frenzied work on a series of exploratory burrows, bringing gasps of alarm from the girl's pale lips. Alarm gives way to resignation when she is pulled sharply back into her master's body, tripping on his feet as they reverse out of the room and disappear into the hall. A stair creaks. A door closes. Above.

Maintaining the visceral wheeze and gurgle of his snores, the duplicitous guest arises from his chair, tiptoes over to the desk, and slides open the main drawer. Nothing. Drawer after drawer, silently opened and closed. Documents methodically flicked through. When something takes his fancy, he photographs it with a miniature camera. His ears strain to catch the sound of approaching footsteps. Nothing. Nothing but the faint moans and the creaking of floorboards overhead.

Desk finished with, he scans the bookshelves.
Meredith, Moore, Trollope and a host of other nineteenth-century bores fill the shelves of a complete wall. He draws out one dusty volume from

a set of Ruskin. '*Ex Libris. Sir Arthur Admetus.*' On the wall next to the open door are sections on Classical History, Greek and Roman Literature, Heretic Philosophy. From the family collection. Undisturbed for decades. The shelves surrounding the liquor cabinet however, are of a more contemporary and... Ahaa!... personal interest. On high, top shelf, the detritus from the great man's undergraduate career – critical studies of Milton, Dryden, Pope, Blake. Lower, third shelf down, amid a jumble of Orczies and Wheatleys, he spots a dozen slender volumellas entitled '*The Restoration of Dryden – Myth and Progenesis*' by Harold Admetus'. He resists the less-than-overpowering urge to peruse, and turns his attention to the books below. Three shelves of Canonical Discourse, firmly Anglo-Catholic in flavour, plus modern editions of all the Oxford Movement favourites, Newman before The Fall, Pusey, Keble, et al.

But on the bottom shelf... something more unusual...
a phalanx of ponderous antiquarian texts with ragged black and gold spines. Some of the titles even he has heard of. *Codex Ebnerianus*. *Queen Melisande's Psalter*. What are these gems of mediaeval book illustration doing here? About to withdraw the Psalter, his attention is lured to the other end of the shelf. One of the books is leaning forward from the ranks of its fellows. *The Principles Of Sacerdotal Hegemony*.
He pulls it out. Pauses. Listening.
Still the moans from the upper room.
The book feels light in his hands, too light.

He runs his fingers over the crisp leather tooling of its front cover. Inside, the pages have been glued together and a rectangular hole cut out. The resulting frame has been fixed to the backboard to form a secret box. In the box, a heap of shiny polaroids.

The phoney pedlar's phoney gut freezes over.
Stripped bodies, faces, flashlit up-close in ivory and molasses.
Waif faces, eyes drugged into craters, staring out at him, beyond
care, and outside the faces, a vagueness of beaten limbs, held down
and pulled apart. Selves, genders... all lost.
The brandy in his stomach churns and boils.
Under the polaroids, a memory stick, unlabelled.
Into his pocket.

He shuts the fake book. Fumbles it back into place. Remembers he
should be snoring, and all but swallows his tongue, which has gone
numb between his teeth. Front half of it seems missing. Raises
forearm to mouth. Opens his lips. Wets his sleeve. No blood.

From the room above –
a scuffle. A stifled ejaculation.
A couple of minutes and they'll be down.
He glances into the hall and notices an exceptionally tall wardrobe,
knobbled all over with florid black carving. He tiptoes across and
prises open the locked doors. Purple lava floods down from the dark
interior, along with a familiar smell. Incense. He pulls aside the long
silk robe, and finds three more of the same. Looks up. As he thought.
The lapels are trimmed with gold-starred ermine. The Archbishop.
Pontifex Maximus. Either living here, with Admetus. Or...

He clicks shut the doors,
carefully, and is answered
by the click of a doorcatch upstairs.

Back in the study,
spiralling down into the armchair,
he resumes the snore. But quiet, settled.

A gentle slap-slap.
Small feet, on a tiled floor.
'Kh..kh..k..' Three coughs from a small throat.
Theatrically, with finger and thumb, he cranks up his right eyelid. Han,
the maid, younger than he first thought, waits in the doorway, eyes puffy,
brow damp and flushed. 'Professor say you have... Here fifty pound, sir.
You have dusters?'
Brownie jumps to his feet, grabs a handful of dusters from his tray, places
them on the desk before the girl and relieves her of the fifty. 'Listen. I'm
not what you think,' he hisses. 'Come with me now. I know somewhere
safe. Trust me. He'll never find you.'
She stands rigid. 'No, no,' lips barely moving, 'he... '
She takes the dusters and backs out of the room.
'No, sir. Must go now. Thankyou, sir – please go.'

Picking up his tray and looping the straps over his head and shoulders,
he follows her into the hall. At first she seems to have vanished. But then
he spots her, in an alcove under the stairs, cowering behind a japanese
aralia, one of a clump of exotic plants crowded into an earth-filled stone
sarcophagus. On the container's side is a picture sculpted in high relief of
an antlered man being attacked by dogs.

Something hard and wet strikes him on the cheek,
rolls along the tiled floor.

He looks up and sees Admetus scowling down at him from the balcony, seated on the banister with his head lolled back against the wall. One leg is stretched out along the handrail. Taking a torn strip of card from his dressing gown pocket, the professor stokes it into his mouth, chews on it for a while, rolls it into a ball, and flicks it at his guest. A timely jerk of the head causes the missile to pass by.

'Something private, you said?'

Brownie pulls himself together.

'Elixirs, guvnor. Customised elixirs, all mixed up accordin to yer own private star sign. Inside each bottle's a unique an amazin potion learnt from the likes of Confucius an Nostrydamus, an all the other great slitty-eyed sages of the Orient. Proved over the centuries as efficacious in relievin the symptoms of all nervous an physical disorders, as well as ...'

Another soggy pellet whizzes by.

'Get out, shyster! Vamoose!'

Brownie glances at the maid,

who shakes her head at him.

'Out!'

'Just goin guvnor. If you're sure...'

'OUT!'

Fast as he can,

hampered by his heavy tray,

the ersatz cockney pulls open the front door

and stumbles out into the night.

tab: 30

in which Brownie continues his sub rosa researches

11 p.m.
A fresh burst of rain.

Shelter. Carapaced
by a low-skirted yew,
before the house of
Woofie and Tinkerbelle.

Trebizond Close.
No 7, open-doored,
suppurating light into light.

The intervening boughs sag with dripping leaves.
His feet are cold, his shoes soaked in the long grass.

The ambulance and its flashing cobalt
have been here for ten minutes.
Big umbrellas semicircle the cottage.
Two paramedics emerge carrying a stretcher.
The face of the motionless invalid is
hidden by a cloud-filled respirator.

In the cottage doorway. A storm of pink lace. A screeching noise.
'*Nono-o-o-o...!*' Tinkerbelle, prevented from running after the stretcher
by a third man in uniform. 'Sorry, my love,' he purrs, 'your brother's had

another stroke,' – slamming shut the rear doors – 'It's urgent and you'll
only get in the way,' – patting the sobbing sister's arm before climbing up
into the driving seat. 'We'll send a car to collect you in an hour or so.'

To the head-wrecking bray of its siren,
the orange and yellow machine
jerks forward, takes a breath,
and lunges off
into the night.

The door of No. 7 closes.
The sobbing relents.
The rain stops.

tab: 31

which further recounts the story of Brownie's eventful evening

11.15 p.m.
Bishopric Square.
Morticed into the west-facing
shell of the Old Bishop's Palace,
a small half-timbered cottage.
A shiny door.
A fanlight number. 2B.

Acridity. Slick maroon.
Fresh paint. He tests it,
near the keyhole, little finger.
Dry. And the doorpost. Dry.
'THE SECRETARY : STRICTLY PRIVATE'
Presses the illuminated doorbell.
Steps back. Nothing.
No glimmer from inside.

He turns slowly around to face the cobbled piazza. A dog's breakfast of
ill-matched relics. Fenced-in bits of Saxon transept, eighteenth-century
almshouses, renovated Tudor cottages, bungled neo-Georgiana. And
all presided over, from the centre, by the cranky midwives of Axtonian
Anglo-Catholicism:
Constantine, bronze.
Augustine, bronze.
Pusey, bronze.

He rubs the back of his neck, still sore from the leather straps.
Glad he's binned the whole caboodle. Served its purpose.
Moves along the cottage wall to an uncurtained window.
Peers into an empty room. Old paint crumbles under his touch.

A short walk down a covered passageway brings him to the cottage's backyard. Darker here, overhung by a cliff of deserted ecclesiastical offices, and in the yard itself, a lumpy ziggurat of cardboard boxes and white polystyrene. He vaults over the low fence, circles the pile of packaging, and examines the labels by means of a key-ring torch. Kitchen equipment, Italian, very posh, presumably awaiting installation indoors. 'Somebody's shelling out a fortune in leaked offertories by all that's bloody wonderful...' He rattles the back door. Considers breaking in. No. Fed up with silly voices and make-believe, he plucks off his bald scalp, peels away the latex nose, drops both into a pocket of his seedy herringbone, and pulls out a cloth, followed by a tube of cold cream.

Back under the streetlight,
he looks at his watch.
Time, after all.
For the last visit.

And off he ambles,
a lanky arachnid,
to the darkest,
farthest corner
of the Square.

tab: 32

in which Brownie calls on Mrs Creech

11.35 p.m.
Trebizond Close. No 52. Inside.

'Ooooh, Mr Turrentine, I am shocked. Who'd have thought it? Poor old
Woofie. No, you're right he's not dead yet so we mustn't talk as if he was.
A second stroke is bad though, at his age. The oldest he was, sorry, is, by
five minutes, and his sister dotes on him. She'll be beside herself, poor girl.
A lovely house they've got, as I'm sure you know.
But ten years younger than me... O my goodness.'

He brings the glass of British sherry to his lips. The woman shuffles
round behind him, tainting the air with a slight whiff of incontinence.
Methodically, feather duster in hand, she is giving a good going-over to
the Creech library. Left to right, top to bottom. Books come out in
handfuls and dustclouds are dismissed from their upper quarters with a
flick of her flounced baton. Brownie turns around on the sofa. Even
sitting, his head is barely lower than hers. Banalities glurp unstoppably
from the corseted body. He notes with displeasure the greasy tails of
dyed black hair barcoded across her ivory scalp, and the tiara of tight
black curls crawling like a centipede round to the back of her neck. A
close-fitting white chemise, belted at the waist into a pair of over-
stretched beige slacks, gives her the look of a peeled breakfast egg
cooling in its wooden eggcup. He urges himself to focus, trusting that
somewhere in the inundation of galactic semolina there will come
floating by, sooner or later, if he's patient, the odd gob of sweet red jam.

146

'I dread telling James, I really do. The Creeches and the Dears have always been friends, but he's got really fond of Woofie since the poor chap had his first stroke must be two years ago now. Takes his chess set round to their house once a week to give him a game. Not many can beat my James at chess, Mr Turrentine, but he always lets him win. Gives him such pleasure to see the old boy's face light up when he thinks he's won. But that's my James. Too soft for his own good. Thank goodness he's got an employer who relies on him or I don't know where we'd be. I know he gets well paid, but the times I've heard him slaving away all night for the blessed Dean. Locked himself in his room for three days once and I know he was working all the time because whenever I passed his door I could hear the rustle of papers or the beep-beep of his blooming computer. Parliamentary Audit, that's what it was. Long time ago now so you probably don't remember. Some silly journalist and a couple of politicians kicking up a fuss over Securicom profits, or Axton Electric as it was then, on a Ministry of Defence contract. That put the cat among the jolly pigeons I can tell you. Two o'clock in the morning the Dean called here in a right state banging on the door like the very devil and terrifying the life out of us. A big argument there was. James called it unprofessional and I know he hated doing it, but the Dean said it was for the Guild and the Church and so on, and that's why he did it in the end I suppose. I know I shouldn't be going on like this of course, but we don't get many visitors and I don't get out much because of my feet and I know I can trust you because James has sort of said so. He's a good boy to me really and I've no right to complain but I do wish he wouldn't spend so much time away. I'm a home body, Mr Turrentine. I like to see different places and different people and in our younger days me and Mr Creech were great walkers, but home is where the heart is when all's said and done and there's no place like it. I love to have my own things around me to keep clean and nice and my own comfy chair to sit in, but all the same it gets very boring with no-one to talk to and I really look forward to James coming home of an evening. So it doesn't seem right that his voluntary gubbins at the Cathedral keeps him out and leaves me all alone by myself so much. You poor thing, you – having to listen to me chuntering on – but you see what I mean, it's gone eleven and he's still not back. But don't go thinking he doesn't love me. Indeed I know he does and he's very kind and generous to his old mum in his own special way. Most boys his age can't wait to flee the nest and leave their parents to fend for themselves, but I've been on my own since dear Alfred died of a growth all those years ago, and I raised him all by myself since he was eight, so I feel these things more than most. And I need the company you understand. Second night this week it is he's been out at the Cathedral, fiddling around in the bookshop whilst here I am, waiting for him all by myself with his dinner spoiling in the oven. And now you're waiting for him too. Oh, are you going already, Mr Turrentine? I'm so sorry James wasn't here, but you can see how things are now.

Think nothing of it, dear. And yes, I'll tell him you called. And thank you ever so much for dropping in. It's been a real pleasure having a natter with another living soul, I can tell you.

That's right, love, you wrap up warm.

Goodnight, Mr Turrentine,
and God bless.'

tab: 33

which observes an unorthodox surgical procedure
enacted upon the older twin

Etherised, 3.00 a.m.,
upon a silver counter,
the land lies naked.
Subcutis, neath skin,
nigh angle of mandible,
jaw of dreaming subject,
jugular of Woofie Dear,
his insect pulse, insect wing...

...once-upon-a once-upon-a once-upon-a land of faraway blue castles and pastel-washed pebbles, pebbles, pebbles that melt-into melt-into an-an-an-an-an-in-a certain village in a certain valley-valley-alley-alley dwel-el-el-el-el-elt a farmer-armer who was neither-either-neither-either rich-ich-ich nor-nor cunning-ing-ing-ing-ing-g-g-g... hoooo-hoooo-hoooo laughed at him and called him Farmerling-ing-a-gaga-gaga... No-no-not No-no-no-not a single cow did he o-o-o-o-o-o-o-o-own... wi-wi-wife wife he said to her-er-er er-er-er, make us a calf-alf-alf out of wood-ood-ood and paint it brown-own-ownnn, ennnnn? ennnnn? aaaannnnn? ennn nnnn? aaaan become a live cow-cow-cow? ...aaaa aaaa an-and thus thus the wooden calf was made and-and-and painted and fashioned in such wise, that its head-ead-ead-ead-ead-ead-ead-ead-ead-ead-ead-ead-ead-ead-ead-ead-ead-ead-ead-ead-ead-ead-ead-ead-ead-ead-ead-ead-ead-ead-ead was bent down as if eating...

Capped.
Masked.
Erect. In silentio.
Around the subject await
six white-cassocked celebrants.
A seventh, discovered peripherally, in orange,
organizes steelware on a surgical trolley.
An eighth, discovered peripherally, in orange,
balances the dials on a pair of gas cylinders.
A ninth, apparelled in forest green, enters the room and flounces across
the tiled white space to assume authority at the head of the subject, in
a gap reserved for him by the encircling fellowship.
Green cap, green mask,
green gloves and overshoes;
green man. Green George.
'Salvete, boys and girls! Heavens, what a great leveller is the surgical
mask. One might almost imagine oneself among equals, instead of...
exempli gratia, let's see... numero, aah, thirty, aah, SEVEN!'
Labelled specimen Thirty-seven steps forward.
'Curriculum vitae if you please,' smiles down his lofty green gauleiter.
'SssAH!... Reference Number Thirty-seven on secondment to the
scheme from Secure Unit Five, Dartmoor Extension. Volunteered by
the Governor. Tangential lobotomy sponsored by private donation
and performed by yourself, sir, using the cold laser technique.
Cashiered ex-lieutenant, 3rd Dorset Rifles. Served eight of thirty for
armed robbery and attempted murder. Victim regrettably paralysed.
Three years in Study Section, sir, gaining an O.U. First in Ethics and
Neuropathology. Number Thirty-seven, three seven, in A1 condition,
eager to learn and ready for work... SssAH!'
Thirty-seven rejoins the circle...

...en-n-next morning, as-as his neighbours' cattle were were were were being driven to pasture, Farmerling hailed a passing herdsman-an-an-an-an a little calf so weak-eak-eak it can barely stan-an-an-and... it must have grass or I fear it will die-die-die-die-die-die-die-die-die-die-die-die-diedie-die-diedie-die-die-die-die-die-die-die-die-die-die-die-die-die-diedie die-die-die-die-die-die-die-die-die-die-die-die...so-so-so, so-so-so...an-an-an... stan-an-an-anding up-up-up in-in-in my-my-meadow eating my-my grass all day-day-day...day-day...da-da-da...da-da-da...da-da-da...da-da-da...da-da-da...da-da-da...da-da-da...da-da-da...

The pristine theatre holds its breath as Green George arms himself with sharp steel and directs a nod to the foot of the table, where Fifty-three, one of the two orange technicians, is braced over a small control panel. He returns the nod and flicks a switch, causing the naked and comatose Woofie, arms clamped to sides, to be lifted in iron claws from the table and inverted 180 degrees like a spit-roast chicken...

...an-an en-en Farmerling-ing met herdsmen driving cattle in the village without his wooden calf-alf he-hee-eeeeeee...where-where-where's my calf-alf? Still-still-still eating my grass-grass-ass-ass-ass-ass-aass-aasssssssss but the little calf was gone-gone-gone gone-gone-gone on-on-on an-an sssss-sssss-sssss-sssss-so sssss-sssss-sssss-so sssss-sssss-sssss-so sssss-sssss-sssss-so angry-angry sssss-sssss-sssss-so angry-angry-angry before the mayoress-sss-sssss-sssss-so who was-as-as-as-as sssss-so so angry and ordered him to give his poor neighbour a whole live cow in compensation...

Back of head,
spine of subject,
gluteal heathland - all in level plane.

From a loudspeaker secreted in a corner of the whited sepulchre
seeps an ululation which grows in volume to a drumroll.
The sixfootsix green phenomenon
pirouettes away from the subject
and shuts his eyes as an elasticated blindfold
is slipped into place between cap and mask.
Scalpels flash under multiple suns.
Hands cross over wrists,
over arms, over head.
Drumroll reaches crescendo.
A whizzing diaphanous tornado
spins towards the subject's top end.
'YEEEEE,' it screams, 'hAAAAW!'
And brakes,
scalpels poised one inch
above the subject's necknape.
Silence. As. As.
Flick of wrist
snickers open
a short furrow
across the shaved muscle...

...ing-ing and his wife were hap-ap-appy now they had a real live cow.
But with... But with... But with such... cannot-not-not feed their live cow
and it grew-grew-woooo-woooo-oooo-oooo-oooo thin-thinner and thin-
thin-thinner and e-eeee-eeee-eeee-eeee-eeee-eeee-eeee-eeee-eeee- to-to-to-to...
kill-kill-kill-kill... it-it-it-it... and r-r-r-r-r-r-r-r-r-r-r-r-r-r-r-r-r-r-r-r-
r-r-r-r-r-r-r-r-r-rolled up the dried cowskin, bade farewell to his wife,
an-an-an an-an-an an-an-an an-and set off to sell it in-in the town...

'Bradawl!' demands Green George.

With the wound prised wide and clipped open by Thirty-seven,
the blindfolded surgeon places the flat point of a bodkin chisel against
the exposed upper brainstem and taps the stock with a rubber mallet.
Held rigid by clamps and claws,
Woofie's body convulses a full minute...

...a-a-a-a-as-as-as-as-as-as-as-as-as-as-as-as-as-as-as-as-as-as-as-as-as-as
an-an-an-an-an-an-an-the sun grew hot an-an-an-an-an-an-an-an-an
the stones cra-cra-cra-cra-cra-a-a-cked and burst into flame...an-on-an
upturned cart... a rook-ook-ook with a sick-ick-icky wing... He lifted the
bird to wrap-ap-ap-ap-ap-ap-ap-ap-ap -ap-ap-ap-ap-ap-ap-ap-ap-ap-
ap-ap-ap-ap-ap-ap-it in the cowskin and fed-fed-fed-it his last piece of
bread-ead-ead-ead-ead-ead-ead-ead-ead-end-en-en-en-en-en-en-en en-
en-on-en-on-en-on-en-on-en-on Farmerling's shoulder...

'Blindfold, Thirty-seven.'

Blindfold is removed.

'Q.E.D. - P.V.S. - P.D.Q. - Und so?'

Tutor group re-convenes.

Surgeon elucidates:

'Und so. P.V.S. equals Persistent Vegetative State.

This is what occurs when (a): the cerebral cortex is functionless due
to extensive damage to its ascending and descending fibres, or because
of anoxic neocortical necrosis, and when (b): the inner brainstem and
deep sub-cortical structures are left intact so that breathing and a small
range of reflex responses are possible...

Questions?'

       Ping...

He glances down at his handiwork
as Thirty-five bends over the incision
with a pair of stitching pliers.
'What I can do blindfold in twenty seconds, you will learn to do in
twenty minutes.   Otherwise... it's a turn on the table... sans
anaesthetic...
Questions?'
        Ping...
Red-and-wet
dribbles down
the jaw of subject,
drips off chin, adam's apple,
into a steel kidney bowl.
        Ping...
        Ping...

*...ith-ith the rook-ook-ook on his shoulder, Farmerling-g-g-g-ag-ag-ag-ag
to the merchant for thirty ducu-cucu-cucu-cucu-cucu-cucu-cats-an-an-an-an-
an-an-an-an-an-an-an-an-an-an... a healthy little calf-alf-alf and
lots of hay to feed it with-ith-ith-ith 'k-caw...k-caw, k-caw... k-caw, k-
caw... k-caw, k-caw... k-caw, k-caw... k-caw, k-caw... k-caw,' said the
rook-ook-ook and it so hap-ap they were eee-eee-eee- eee-eee-eee- eee-eee-
eee-stood a wooden calf-f-f-f-f-f-f-f-f but-ut-ut-ut cru-cru-cru-crudely
car-car-carved ...ing-ing-ing-ing-ing-ing-ing-ing-ing r-r-r-gar-gar-a-a-
a-a-a-a-a-a-a-a-a-a-a-a-a-a-a-a-a-a-a-a-a-a-a-a-a-a-a-a-a-a-a-a-a-a-a-
a-a-a-a-a-a-a-a-a-a-a-a-a-a-a-a-a-a-a-af-f-f-f-f-fut-ut-ut-ill-ill-ill-ill-
ma-ma-m-m-m-ma-ma-ill-ill-ill-m-m-m-a-a-a-m-m-m-m...*

The surgeon yawns,
peels off gloves,

drags down mask,
lights up stumpy cheroot,
and peruses the tutor group
through a tunnel of concentric smoke rings.
'Reasonably healthy if somewhat aged male, as you see. Severe ischaemic stroke, three to four hours ago, sustaining extensive anoxic neocortical damage with an eighty per cent fucked-up motor system and a five per cent chance of remission. Malheureusement for us but not for him, brainstem necrosis is too profound for the scheme's L.I.S. trigger treatment to work.
So. Ping equals... Pong. Nota Bene.
And L.I.S. equals... Locked-In Syndrome -
which is, please note, what occurs when selective brainstem damage destroys the motor system but spares the arousal mechanisms, leaving the patient fully conscious but unable to communicate. Blinking and vertical eye movement are usually unaffected and the patient can, if necessary, be taught to communicate by code. If necessary...
Questions?'

       Ping...

...ing-ing's w-wi-wife w-w-was indee-dee-dee-dee ve-ve-ve-ve-very an-an-an-an-an-an-an-an-an-an-an-an-an-ah shabby wooden calf-alf an-an-an-an-an-an-an-an-an-an-an-ah-ah-ah hungry rook to fee-ee-ee-ee-ee-ee-ee-ee-ee-ee-ee-ee-ee-da-da-swell-well-well an-an-an-an-an-an-an noo-oo-oo-oo-oo-oo-oo-oo-oo-oo-oo-oo-oo-oo-oo-oo-oo-overanoveranoveranoveran-over...poor-no-more...poor-no-more...poor-por -por-por-or-or-or-or-or-an-an-an-as it-it-it van-an-anished tha-tha-than a splendid heifer of solid-id-id go-go-go go-go-go g-g-g-g-g-g-g-g-g-g-g-g-g-g-g-g-g-g-g-g-g-g-g-g-g go-go-go go-go-go g-g-gold...

'So, boys and girls, that's the way it is. Sonny Jim here will be with us for no more than two months, when he'll be switched off before renal degradation affects the plasma quality. But as for now, it's straight...' - the surgeon pauses to crush the smouldering stub of his cheroot onto Thirty-three's cotton-capped cranium - '... straight to a rack in the Milking Parlour Ante-room, along with twenty others, all rather less fortunate than him and all treated with our own brand of surgically induced Locked-in Syndrome. Questions?'

Ping...

...en-en-en-en-en-when the rich-ich-ich la-la-la la-la-landowners of the valley-valley-alley wer-er-e-er-er-er-er-er-er-er-er three thousand ducats eee-eee-eee-eee-eee-eee-eee-eee-eee-eee-eee-eee-eee-eee-eeeee eeee-each-oh-no-noo-noo-noo-noo-noo-noo-noo-noo-noo-noo-noo-no- more than half a-a-a-a-a-a-a-a-a-a-a-a-a-a-a-a-a-a-a-a-a-a-a-a-a-a-a-a-a-a-a-a-a- a-a-a-a-a-a-a-a-a-a a-a-a-a-a-a-a-a-a-a-a-a-a-a-a-a-a-a-a-a-a-a-a- a-a-a-a-a-a-a-a-a-a-a-a-a-a-a-a-a-a-a-a-a-a-a-a...

'Any questions?'

...an-an na-a-a-a-a-a-a-a-a-a-a-a-a-a-a-a-a-a-a-a-a-a-a-a-a-a-a-a- tha-tha-tha-tha-tha-tha-tha-tha-tha-tha-tha-tha-tha-tha-tha-tha-tha-tha -all-all-all-alla-alla-alla-alla-all-all-all-a-ruined ug-ug-ug-eeeeecchh ug-ug-ug-ug-eeeecchhhhhh-ug-ug-ug-eeecch the-ri-chich-ichest-in-in-in-the-realm-umm-umm-umm-ummah a-a-a-a-a-a-a-a-a-a-a- a-a-a-a-a-a- a-a-a-a-a-a-a-a-a-a-a-a-a-a-a-a-a-a-a-a-a-a-a-a-a-a-a-a-a-a-a -a-a-a-a-a-a-a-a-a-a-a-a-a-a-a-a-a-a-a-a-a-a-a-a-a a-a-a-a-a-a- a-a-a-a-a-a-a-a-a-a-a-a-a-a-a-a-a-a-a-a-a-a-a-a-a-a-a-a-a-a -a-a-a-a-a-a-a-a-a-a-a-a-a-a-a-a-a-a-a-a-a-a-a-a...

'Any questions at all?'

'Hunnn...
...hunnnngh?'
A bashful enquiry?
'Hu... unnnNNNNGH?'
- from the throat of the subject?
The blood-run features
are skewing into ...can it be?
twisting into ...can it be?
...a scOWL? ...a smIRK? ...a wINK!!!?

Thirty-nine, well, shrieks, as...
            Ping...
Forty hits the floor in a deadfaint, as...
            Ping...
Thirty-five stabs her thigh with a needle, as...
            Ping...
Thirty-seven tippy-toes backward to the exit, as...
            Ping...
Thirty-eight bites clean through his lower lip, as...
            Ping...
Forty-one feels a hot yellow cataract filling her shoes, as...
            Ping...

'And nota bene this also,' beams Green George. 'With P.V.S., a flinching
of the spastic limbs away from pain and a grasp reflex when the fingers
are stroked are sometimes mistaken for signs of returning consciousness.
But the most careful examination will reveal no intellectually

meaningful response, none at all, and although grimacing and groaning
noises may occur, no intelligible sound is ever uttered...
Still no questions?'

The spit rolls.
The claws return the body
to its place on the table.

On the mouth
of the subject
a pink-veined bubble
swells,
             shivers,

pops.

tab: 34

which observes the wretchedness of the younger twin

Trebizond Close, 3.30 a.m.
No. 7. Inside.

Scuffle of padded coathangers.
A short drop to the baseboard.
Crack of snapped ulna as an outflung arm
breaks the backblade of a nearby chair.

Waking, she finds herself propped in
joke languor against the trouser press.
From a gash in her right hip
blood seeps down her thigh
into the soft white salubrity
of the bedside rug.

Collared in fire,
heretic in a
cult of pain,
she stands, slowly,
coaxes her fingers
to find again the
ends of the rope.

Climbs her gallows.
For one more try.

tab: 35

which concludes the account of Brownie's nocturnal investigations
with a small fire and an apparent suicide

Trebizond Close, 3.30 a.m.
No. 7. Outside.

Twenty minutes, under the yew.
Looking up at the bedroom window.
At the movement on its nectarine skin.
Trying to make sense of the knocks,
and creaks, and exhalations.

The streetlights die.
Somewhat premature, thinks Brownie.
And not only the streetlights.
Power cut, thinks Brownie.
Glimmer on the black window.
Candle, thinks Brownie.
Thump.
The glimmer dies.
And revives,
strengthening
to a fiery glare.

The door splinters underfoot.
He falls into pitch. Skates blind across a polished floor.
Bumps into, grabs banisters. No smoke yet. Takes stairs three at a time.

Small landing. Smoke. Crashes into a room. Gags on carbon.
Stung eyes make out a smoky glow, centre stage.
Fire, in a waste bin.
Already burning itself out.

Bedroom.
Twin beds. Wardrobe. Dressing table.
He stands still, listening. Feathers of soot tickle his nose.
A willie-winkie nightlight has toppled into the bin from the dressing table and, perversely, is still upright and alive among the embers. Avoiding the flame, he lifts the candleholder and sets it down before the expansive oxbow of the dressing table mirror.

Neither bed has been slept in.
Across the end of one, a nightdress has been laid.
A breeze shoulders its way through the chintz curtains,
snuffing out the candle.

He pulls a book of matches from an inside pocket and re-ignites the wick. With the candle held high, he surveys the dim chamber and is about to explore the rest of the house when he notices a barely perceptible but regular opening-and-shutting of the wardrobe door. Two inches, widening to four, and back again.
Then a muffled clicking, synchronised to the swings of the door.

He edges the candle forward. The light is too weak.
Overriding the sourness of sulphur, burnt paper and candlegrease, comes another smell from inside the wardrobe, sweet, sickly, faecal...

His left hand moves to the brass doorknob.
His right hand, holding the candle,
shakes uncontrollably.
A slug of wax-melt plops onto his bare wrist.

The mirrored door bursts open, ripping screws off hinges,
cartwheels into the dressing table, shatters glass into glass.
A stem of braceleted arm punches out from above, flails downward,
dragging diamonds and fingernails through the flesh of his cheek.

At a strange angle to its neck, the head of Tinkerbelle Dear nods at him
with a guarded dogleg smile. Her shoulders twitch continually as if
bothered by a tickle, or persistent fly.

The summer-frocked body is once again racked by spasm, limbs thrown
into dithyrambic farce before returning to their former, gentler, agitation.
Liquid rust dribbles down the naked feet, off the toes,
onto the blue encyclopaedias of her gallows platform.

He replaces the candle and leans forward,
hugs and lifts the tiny waif body,
unhooking the rope from the wardrobe ceiling.
Is the trembling his or hers? The stench his or hers?
He lays her on the bed.
Dead. And despite
fitting his mouth to
hers and blowing hard,
stinking dead she remains.

Out.
Get out.
Out and down.
Down the dark stairs.
Don't stumble.
Leave the broken bitch.
Shut the broken door.

Narrow. Spiteful.
Bitters for blood.
Good riddance.

Smacksmack,
feet on pavement.
Counting the steps home,
he watches with interest
as the brown of his boots
reclaims itself from
the oatmeal blur
of concrete.
He recalls
lightness,
frailty.

Overhead, above the roofs,
against a softening sky,
the streetlamps rekindle
into chrome yellow life.

tab: 36

in which Clarissa and the Dean are descried in flagrante delicto

7.00 a.m.

The Bishop's Palace.

Breath...

Clouds...

Glass...

The anonymous author of 'The Xiomögion', that unjustly neglected eleventh-century omnium gatherum of Saxon legends, began it all. His description of the Mercian kingdom of Wenydd as a 'Land of Fear and Enchantment' was perhaps the earliest attempt to portray in writing the unique natural beauty of this eastern outpost of the Celtic diaspora. Although, to the great majority of present-day ramblers, this is an exhilarating landscape of rolling moorland, wooded valleys, and moss-capped hills, it was by no means always seen as such. Indeed, the first educated travellers to this land were struck with terror as they cautiously made their way, using guides from the local peasant stock, into these 'horrid and evil places'. One such visitor was Daniel Defoe, in whose book 'A Tour through the Whole Island of Britain' the region is described as 'the most barren and frightful of any I have passed over'. There even now exists a sizeable minority of otherwise intelligent people who see in these airy heights and secluded vales only a sinister malignancy, a perfect arena for malfeasance, carnal turpitude, and every shade of diabolic abomination. Decades of tourism and televisual familiarity have largely inured the modern visitor to such fears, but on a winter's dusk the mist swirling around the twin peaks of Hardrigg and Priddaw can still cause a jolt of panic strong enough to stop the lone rambler in his tracks. In more temperate months however, the smooth steeps of the Northern Domes, moulded from pre-Ordovician slate, attract many thousands of appreciative tourists who love to rest and picnic in the shelter of the nipple-like Tors. Refreshed and replete, the visitors will then, more often than not, wander southward over the Thirteen Ribs of Min-daw, perhaps lingering awhile on Ap Dolmen's crest before finally dropping down to the verdant fertile slopes of Maedendale.

Borne on an uprush of air, the ballooned-out plastic bag of a well-known chain of high street opticians focuses a wide wrinkled eye on the grassy knoll of Ap Dolmen, at the centre of which is a shallow depression filled with the brightly coloured anoraks of more than a hundred people. The object of their attention is Eve's Well, a cavernous pothole augured into the pink slate by centuries of ice and rain. The anoraks are pressing forward, tossing coins down its deep black gullet.
A sudden mist descends. Fold on fold of hung drizzle.
The plastic yellow eye crackles and turns in the breeze,
sees a small dark-suited figure detach itself from the group.
Male. Urgent atomic.
Wolf-spider, compact.
Or. Human-faced fly.
The eye closes in.
Closes in. Closes in.
The fly-human scuttles south,
over hillocks and hollows,
and hillocks, and hollows.
Scuttles south over moor
and mere and soft-laid land.

Comes to trees and grazing-orchards;
cressbeds, meadows; a strawberry field.
And south again past farms and churches
to the open country, and hills and
haunch-hills, and ridges long like thighs.
A centre-star of thighs,
where a man in navy pyjamas -
'O Christ, Clarr,'
- stalks amity and pleasure.

'O bury me in flesh, germana cara...
O queen of heaven, regina caeli...
Drown me in your hot milk...
Laetare...
Lactesco, lactesco...
Suck me in through the
pores and mouths of your hot flesh.'
The land heaves, chuckling as her
lover's teeth draw blood from belly
and his bony fingers twist
beads of milk from her breasts.
In the calix of his need
the lover's prick
stirs aromatic soup,
rubs head against red wall,
seeks admission to the womb.
'Tell me, Clarr.'
'What?' she sniggers.
'First time. With the farmer.'

'The horse-box?'
'Yesss!'
'Say please.'
'Please, Clarr... Please?'

Outside the window,
unnoticed by the bedded copulars,
booted feet snap branches from a gnarled wisteria.
Hands grab for sill. Fingernails scrape glass,
rake putty from casement.

As rivulets of eye-blue lava
crisscross the flanks of the land,
the lover moves among them
in a waft of lavender,
undisturbing thrip
or grasshopper,
gathering pollen dust to the brushed viyella
of his pyjama bottoms, grazing with his lips
the freckled pinkness of the lea,
laying hands on molemounds,
tasting salt, entering once more
the coppice in the vale.
Above his head
knives of ash-leaf
flash and clash.
At his feet the shoots
of day-old bracken
wait like curled sea horses

to be crushed to pulp.
He plunges, he plunges
to the heart of the wood,
cut by ash wands,
blind in hot blood.

'Oh Clarr....Clarr,' he gasps, as a
long moon of nose-flattened face
presses itself to the window,
as the calves of the woman's legs
encircle him, pull him in deeper.
'Ckccc....'

The face at the window drifts
sideways, behind the curtain.
On the bed,
ruffled by the sense
of a third presence,
the naked non-nurse
grabs a fistful of cotton,
and casts off her lover
like a hank of seaweed.

At the window,
she draws aside the lace curtain, looks down
through the grey morning and the swagged wisteria,
sees a white-headed figure jump to ground
and disappear behind a flint buttress.
'It's Pigeon.'

The Dean Exalted
of the Abbey Cathedral
of Saint Wulfrig-at-Axton
lies spreadeagled on
his open dressing gown,
cock shrinking into pyjamas,
trailing glair on the dark twill.
'He'd have found out anyway, sooner or later.'
'It'll still have to be dealt with,' she sighs,
scratching a rib beneath her left breast.
'Turrentine will know his whereabouts.'
'Turrentine will tell us what suits him.'
'Thought you said he was ok.'
'Used to be. Needs seeing to.'
'Even thought you... sort of, fancied him.'
'O did you?' she squeals.

Stands over the bed.
Doublecreamy. Solid.
Rests a knee on the mattress. Leans forward,
globes of shiny stilton overhanging his face.
'Where's Willy?' she enquires as her good left hand wriggles through his
pyjama fly to greet the aforementioned revivified member with a firm
squeeze. Thus attached, she swings a leg over her lover's chest, knees
clamping the upper arms, cunt over face, descending. 'Pray, Reverend.
Redeem yourself from the dungeons of the flesh.'

'Albighty and bost berciful Farber...' – rucks of labial heat mashing up
words, breath, meaning – '...we hab erred and strayed frob thy ways

like loss schleep. We hab followeb musch ... the... de.. ..bler...de..b... the devices and desireth ob our owb hearth. Vwee hab... ..offended against thy ....by Hobly Lawb'

'O Lord, open thou our lips.
Come on, priest. Any more?'

'Nn our mouff schll shoo froth bly plaithe.'

'Praise ye the Lord, lover. And?...'

'Khh.....k..k..k.'

'Glory be to the Father.'

'...Mmm...bubba.'

'And to the Son.'

'Nnth...th..Bowthly Glosht.'

'As it was in the beginning... is now... and?... and?...'

'Ebber schlell bee.'

'Amen.'

'Arbebb.'

A live hot poultice.
Meal and magma.
Crushing. Stifling.
Disengaging.

'Aaahh... nd...

                    send us,' incants
the immobilised cleric, 'send us...
and send us   we beseech thee
in our necessity,   such moderate
rain and showers   that we may
receive   the fruits   of the Earth to
our comfort   and thine   honour
through Jesu Christ   Ouarrr...
aaahhrr...'

'-pssssSSSS-'
        'Aaahh...'

    '-psssSSSSSS-'
                'Mmmm...'

      '-psssSSSSSSSS-'
              'Aa..aaa..mm...'

          '-pssSSSSSSSSSS-'
                  'Mmm..ENNNNNNNNN...!'

tab: 37

which observes Pigeon in some disarray, and a chance encounter with Kinch

Run,
Pigeon,
run, run
over lawn
and lawn
and lawnspit,
under pergolas,
round the dug beds
of the kitchen garden,
run and run and run
and scramble through

a gap
between
hedge of yew and
StigSoc wall. Damn!...
as the empty sling snags
on a twig. He pulls it free.
Trips on wire.
Totters out into
wet marshgrass.
Over a low fence.
Onto the towpath.

Her voice...
He lifts his mangled arm,
works it back into the sling.
Her voice... the sound of it,
'keep it rested till I see you.'
See you...
Bandage torn. Blood.
Scowls at the grazed
fingertips, one nail bent back
ragged from his grab at the sill.
Turn right. Follow the canal.

They won't come after him.
Seen too much, too much.
Too much. Feet drag gravel.
Canal sneaks by in its ditch,
breathing fever into air.
Gravel demurs to grit,
and grit to a hard shell
of loam and brickdust.
Could jump across.
Islands of turf are offered.
But long leaps are needed.

Ratchet on, dark water.

> *... away and mock time...*
> *... false face must hide...*

Over to his left.
The Wall glistens.
Like new bone.

> *... will have blood they say...*

Drizzle starts, and an eruption,
behind, of babble and laughter.
He bends down, to re-tie a shoelace, sees
three upside-down people catching him up.
An elderly pair, enjoying, apparently,
a joke. Husband hatted tyrolean.
Wife in a jolly three-piece.
And with them a blue-cheeked
younger woman, the audience.
He straightens up, trudges on,
slowly, so they can overtake.
Steps aside onto wet grass.
They pass by on the towpath,
ignoring the small courtesy.
Walk faster... Follow the show...

The wife laughs. Snaps open a polka-dot umbrella -
'...sittin on the beach, n'there were this girl sittin next to us with er fella.
Cryin she were so we arst her what's wrong an she said they ony got
married yesterday n'she'd lost er weddin ring on the beach. She wus ever
so upset so we scratched about in the sand fr'ages lookin for it an then
li'l Davy of all people found it, n'she wus so grateful they wennan

bought im a absolutely normous ice cream but e couldn'eat it cos e wus ony three an it were so hot it melted all over all our fingers. N'other time li'l ol Davy went paddlin in the sea with is socks on an e got into some sinky sand, n'is socks got in such a absolute terrible muddy mess that I said oh throw em away, wunwonnem anymore, so we threw'm into the sea. Anyway, next mornin we went down the beach n'there they wus. Lyin side by side on the sand. The sea'd washed em up. Washed em up all nice n'clean an laid em side by side, all neat n'clean n'side by side. So we picked em up, n'took em ome.'

'Where was that?' asks the younger woman.

'Skegness it were. No. Rhyl.'

Pigeon halts.

Shuts his eyes against

spume and wavethump.

Falls back into warm sand.

The voices float away.

He makes a slow half-turn, looks over the canal, towards the Rec. The goalposts' dry geometry cuts through the haze of drizzle. The voluble trio have left the towpath, crossed the footbridge, and are taking the shortcut over the fields back to Farmtown. He gives them a glance and then moves off himself,

same direction, eyes down,

but unfocussed.

... rank sweat...

...enseaméd bed...

What a... Is she...?

She. Clarissa. She, the world's tormentor, who'd cajoled the Dean to take him out of that wretched school and then got the science teacher sacked. She, the fake nurse, bird-killer, cat-killer, misanthrope, whose coarse laughter had all those years ago echoed down the corridors at night as he lay curled tight with confusion under his bedclothes.

What's he to her... she to him...?

The Dean's sister...?

A clack of boots.

His own. On the footbridge.

Ahead, his view of the three walkers is blocked by another walker, lumbering towards him, an overweight duchess with a coiffure of dense mauve hair rough-hewn to the likeness of a giant whelk, towing a yappy spaniel onto the first slats of the bridge. As they pass by, Pigeon flattens himself against the handrail, wary of canine retaliation for the death of the two mastiffs, but the spaniel doesn't give a hoot and scampers on past, barking and pulling on an ever-extending silver lead.

From the bridge the path continues north before turning right, away from Old Axton, through an overgrown corner of the Recreation Ground, whence it emerges alongside the windowless south wall of Gridmore Gloves. The main building, the Factory, is a five-storey Victorian warehouse, girdled with outhouses and dwarfed on its east side by a huge chimney as tall and wide as a cooling tower. Some distance away and connected to the Factory by a tubular bridge is a modern two-storey redbrick with narrow barred windows and an entrance manned day and night by security guards. This newer building, the Annexe, is hidden from the path and tucked between the Factory and the high walls of Cripps Forge, one of the three derelict heavy engineering plants which, in their heydey, were the drab heart and soul of the Braddock Leyes Estate.

He moves fitfully on, pausing to rest his shoulder on the Factory wall, straining to purge his brain of the ugly ill-matched couple on the bed. Halfway along, one of the steel doors which punctuate the blankness of the Factory wall is flung noisily open. A small figure darts out, slams the door shut, and runs this way.

'Kinch!'
He grabs at, holds onto, a worn denim sleeve.
'What are you doing here?'
Before the boy can answer, the door re-opens and extrudes a security guard. Seeing Kinch detained, the guard marches towards them, all braid and polish, and is about to claim the boy for himself when he recognises Pigeon. 'Oh... Hi...,' he splutters, '...all yours then.' Saluting and nodding, the guard reverses painfully into the edge of the steel door, before slinking back into the Factory.

'What you after?' asks Pigeon.
'Nothing. Or nothing much, anyway. But why all those guards, and why is Mum so touchy about it? She won't say anything because of her job, but I'm sure she knows. I'll find out. I'll show them.'
He takes off his glasses,
cleans them on his T-shirt,
hooks them back over his ears.
A faraway look hardens his face,
his jaw clenching, unclenching.

'Listen, Kinch. Best thing now is for you to go back to your Aunts' and lie low. Give me your flat number and I'll let your Mum know you're ok.'

The boy flicks hair from his eyes
and in doing so dislodges his glasses.
They tumble down his face,
onto the asphalt.
He picks them up.
Re-wipes them.

'Fifty-three...

See you.'

He slips from Pigeon's grasp,
ducks through a gap in the hedge,
and dashes over the playing fields
towards the cricket pavilion
and the big roller.

tab: 38

The Rec. Hulked iron. The roller.
Kinch. The watcher. Waiting.
At last.
      The pocket golem shambles off along the path towards
Farmtown, and is slain behind a garden fence,
                                 end house.
'Sorry Pigeon. Business.'
Edge of field. The boy moves off,
jogging through a bramble passage, a beech wood,
                                 into a clearing.
Trees around short grass, fretted blotted velveteen.
He marches to the middle of a perfect fairy ring,
kicks the head from a toadstool, eyes shut, wishing.

One hour later.

The canal.
One.
He drops onto the first of three diseased elm logs bumped and
rolled into the water as tricky bridge to the west bank towpath.
Canal. Black mucus. Usual level, notwithstanding. He jumps.
Two.   Three.
The bank.
Dough-soft, pea-green.

Along the towpath, past the footbridge.

Marshland.

No-one about.

The Wall closes in.

Then left,

scrambling over stile and stone causeway,

onto the picnic patio below Luther's Feet,

pausing before the broken mantra,

                perspex.

LUTHE   R'S FEET

This ramp of shallow   steps was carved into the Blood Wall b
ighteenth-century mer   chants to allow access to the canal.
therto commercial wate   rway traffic had been forbidden by Royal
arter in order to allow hu   nting parties aboard the King's Barge an
mpeded journey from Windso   r to the Wynchin boar reserves on
e Welsh border. But the reserves   had long fallen into disuse by the
time the Axton merchants, led by   one Luther Loudbelly, goldsmith,
declared that the tortuous route acro   ss Farmtown to the canal was an
bsurd inconvenience and successfu   lly challenged the Charter in the
Court. Their first intention was   to cut a new gateway in the Wall,
but this was viewed, even in   those days, as a great
de   secration of heritage and so, as a   compromise, long shallow steps
we   re carved into both sides of the me   diaeval blockwork. However,
whe   n the railway system was built the   canal became redundant as
a co   mmercial route and so the inner ra   mp, on the city side, was
rem   oved   and the marble ashlar res   tored to its pristine
sheern   ess, leaving this outer ramp as a   reminder of the City of
Axton's   unique history.

Up the long low steps. Onto the Wall.
From the outer rampart he looks across
at the copper domes and spires of Old Axton.
Overtessellated – against light, against nature.
A tarnished sky.

Dropping down into the central gulley,
he walks north, surprised as ever by how dull
and pitted the pink marble is, seen up close.

Half a mile further on finds him over the domed roofage of the Farm.
The elaborate complex is grafted onto the sunless north face of the
Blood Wall and hemmed round on its other sides by an enclosure of
flinted brick. Sole access to the Farm is via the Prison House, and thence
through a labyrinth of underground tunnels and checkpoints. Security is
a lethal overhead canopy of meshed razor-lasers. Progress along the
gulley and ramparts is at this point halted by a steel fence. For a complete
circuit of the Wall, the truly committed hiker must here struggle down
onto a broad ledge carved into the townside flank of the inner rampart.
But Kinch has other plans.

Beyond the Farm and the canal, lies Barley Moor, site of the Celts' final
humiliating stand against the Romans but now said to be so littered with
unexploded mines from its long stint as artillery testing ground that the
ravaged expanse has been a forbidden zone for decades. At one end, the
wall of the military complex adjoins the electrified double barrier
surrounding Barley Moor. Its other end meets the Blood Wall exactly
below the steel endpost of the fence, against which Kinch is now resting.

All quiet, as ever.

Other plans.
He slithers down from the edge of the outer rampart. Lands hard on the
rough coping tiles of the flint and brick wall. With his arms outstretched
for balance, he inches forward, glancing down at the Farm, relieved to
see the security camera still dangling from its pole after last year's gale.
To his right is a triangular patch of rubble,
once the lock-keeper's cottage.
Nearly there.
Above grass now,
he climbs down the brickwork
using footholes hacked into the mortar
by the man he is on his way to see.
He drops the last few feet,
and turns to confront the
acned terrain of the Moor.

A bombed hamlet,
cottages, byres,
a sea of whipped grass,
trees and masonry protruding
like toes of caramelised bone.

He pulls a stopwatch/compass
from his trouser pocket.

10 a.m.
North-north-east.

tab: 39

in which Pigeon seeks to reassure his friend's mother

10 a.m.
Keble Mansions. No. 53.

She stands hunched in the doorway,
wrapped in a man's dressing gown.
From her slight build, her pallor,
her sharp black eyes, Pigeon knows
he's come to the right place.
'My name's Pigeon,' he says.
'Yes, I know,' she whispers back.
'I dropped by to let you know Kinch is staying at his Aunts'. We spoke
about half an hour ago, and he's fine.'
'Thanks. The nurse told me he's at the cottage, but thanks anyway.'
'Kaisa?'
'She called in earlier. Whereabouts... ?'
'At the Rec. He ran off back to his Aunts'. For breakfast, I think.'
'That's good. And very kind of you. Won't you come in for coffee?'
Pigeon declines. Takes his leave.
Down. Clitterclatters down
too many flights of stone stairs.
Cold clammy handrails.
Stench of piss, nicotine.

Outside, he squints up at the sky,
glad of the drizzle on his face as
the door creaks shut behind him.

Forearm hurts. Pulls it out of the sling.
Rewinds the torn linen. The ache sharpens.

He wanders through the streets,
oppressed by the emptiness
and the boarded-up shops.
The sky lightens. Drizzle peters out.
The Hospital must be near.

In front of a steamed-up cafe, a rangy rastafarian is dancing.
Seabed shuffle. Slow. Tideblown. Silent.
Pigeon slips inside, takes a seat by the window and orders tea and a
bacon roll. The bacon is hot lean and crisp, the roll fresh. Warmth
spreads through him, easing the pain in his arm as he idly takes in
the view from the window. Human. Hopeless. Still dancing.

Outside again,
he drops a coin into the dancer's cup and turns down a sidestreet, losing
himself in the maze of alleys and passageways but content in the vague
expectation of coming upon the Hospital.
But not really caring. Not really.

Thirty minutes later he finds himself seated on
a low wall in front of Outpatients, watching
the nurses and the visitors come and go
between the concrete gateposts.
She'll be among them.
She will.

tab: 40

10.30am.
Barley Moor...

360 AD. Summer Solstice.
Twelve thousand painted pikemen –
all wiped out in a single day by a single legion.
And thus it ended, with Gereint of Rhos, Chief of All Celts, shackled,
tonsured, paraded in shame through the streets of Rome and then transported
to the slave cells of Carthage, where a fellow prisoner converted him to
Christianity. As a result of his conversion Gereint was forced to endure a
decade-long ordeal of torture, deprivation and solitude. Finally, in what
seems to have been a petty gesture of contempt for the upstart religion, he was
castrated and pressed into service as official eunuch to the military brothel,
which is where, at the age of thirty-seven, after months of humiliation amid
scenes of the most appalling carnality, he put an end to his sorrows by
repeatedly throwing himself headfirst against a statue of Augustan Dano-
Bacchus, God of Whores and Whoring. A spoonful of his spilled brains was
scraped off the statue by a sympathetic customer and preserved in a glass
bottle. Five centuries later the bottle and its precious contents surfaced in the
Reliquary of Axton Cathedral, where it lies to this day in a casket of lead
and silver. Although the mortal sin of his suicide will always preclude him
from canonization, Gereint was for centuries revered as an 'unofficial'
martyr and right up to the Reformation there are records of his devotees
committing ritual suicide in the manner of their 'saintly' paradigm.

Barley Moor.
A vast pikelet of shallow craters.

Although Kinch knows the unexploded landmines to be a fiction
concocted by the military, and that the whole area was cleared twenty
years ago, the red warning signs are still dotted around and a vestige of
doubt still lingers. So, for the next half mile, until the craters start to thin
out, he keeps to anything even slightly resembling an animal track.
The ground levels as he approaches the bombed hamlet.
First building. A once sizeable cottage or farmhouse,
razed flat except for its stalagmitic chimney breast
complete with hearth, mantel, and a stump of upper flue.

Sun sneaks out from behind a cloud. Stones shimmer and jerk. He halts,
prodding his glasses back up the bridge of his nose. And looks again.

In the tumbledown hearth of the chimney stands a horse,
a marigold palomino with a mane of plaited cream.
Astride its back sits a dark-haired young woman
gowned in silver, shod with buskins of blue cordovan.
On her head, an iron tiara,
encrusted with rubies and emeralds.

She turns to Kinch with a smile of such radiance
that his heart swells in fear, anticipation, desire.

At a touch from her heel the steed heads north.
He sets off to follow, to catch up.
The palomino trots slowly.

He will soon overtake it. He must.
But no. He lengthens his stride,
and even though the horse moves at the same slow gait
the distance between them does not change.
He breaks into a jog, and then a run. No use.
However fast he runs the gap remains,
but still he tries, racked with yearning
at the sight of the maid's hair, rolling
in lovely stormclouds down her back.

She looks at him no more,
but drops out of sight, over
the crest of a large crater.
When he reaches the spot,
the horse and its rider
are nowhere to be seen.
Frantically he explores the pit
for hidden caves or crevices,
but finds nothing, and throws himself
on a bed of turf, weeps bitter tears.

He sobs until his throat aches,
and then he stops,
and then struggles to his feet
clutching for no reason a bendy hazel twig,
which he swipes through the air.

'Ha – HAAAA!'

A voice of thunder bellows out
from behind the charred ruin
of a massive oak tree.

'Ha – HAAAAAAAA!'

Kinch,
as boy knight errant,
mounts an armoured palfrey
which has trotted up beside him.
He takes a shield of leather
and a lance of bright steel
from a nearby weapon rack.
Hoists the lance to perpendicular.
Spurs forward his nimble mare.

From behind the burnt oak steps the figure
of a thick-set yellow-bearded dwarf,
whistling impudently. Under one arm
he holds a fresh-roasted boar. With his free hand
he plucks bristles from the creature's back,
one by one, at incredible speed.
Kinch watches in fascination as the dwarf
sinks his teeth into the boar's belly and
starts chewing on the succulent meat,
warm grease dribbling down his beard.

'Mmmmm... Excellent... Pray excuse me. I am Wrnach Pierce-Thigh,
Samurai of this Domain, yet to be vanquished in any trial of arms or test

of worldly wisdom whatsoever. You, on the other hand, are a coward and
a woodlouse, and a runt from a litter of one. And, furthermore, your
mother is a loony and your father was a coward and a liar and a flea and
a big joke and a ripe pustule on the face of his own stupid memory.'

A donkey appears beside the dwarf,
its back covered by old rugs.
Still clutching the boar under his arm,
he wipes fingers and beard on his chainmail tunic
and leaps onto the donkey. From a close-by copse
he pulls up by its roots a ten foot beech sapling,
bites off the root-end, blows off the twigs,
puts the top-end in his mouth
and sucks it to a sharp point.
This goes under his right arm. His lance.
For shield he uses the half-eaten boar, left arm
rammed elbow-deep up the suidic rectum.
'Ready? Son of a slug?'

They charge.
The lances shatter.
They fight with spears.
When the spears break,
they fight with double-edged swords,
and when the swords break, they fight with maces.
Kinch finds the combat unpleasant because
his opponent is small, and hard to hit,
and deals severe blows.

Mace is followed by battleaxe,
and battleaxe by cutlass.
They do not tire, but their
mounts sink to their knees.
Discarding mounts and shields,
they fall upon each other with dagger and net,
and then with any piece of broken wood or metal they can find.
Helmets are dented, breastplates pierced, chainmail torn.
They fight until both are half-blinded by sweat and blood.

'This is no good,' gasps Kinch. 'I will concede defeat
in return for one trifling favour.'
'And what might that be?' asks Wrnach.
'I have here in my pocket a large bag. If you can fill up this bag with food
from your stores, then victory will be to you alone and you may take
possession of my entire kingdom and all the courtiers and serfs therein.'
'Granted,' says the dwarf.
'A deal,' says Kinch, who draws
a large woven bag from his pocket,
opens it out, and holds it before him, waiting.

The dwarf goes to his stores and returns with a barrel of dry biscuits, but
however many he drops into the mouth of the bag, it remains as empty
as when he started. After the biscuits he tries fruit, throwing in apples
and berries and oranges and even water melons. But still the bag remains
empty. He uses up all his vegetables, all his bread, all his bottles of wine.
In desperation he stuffs a great joint of mutton into the opening and
peers into the bag, but sees nothing but a few grains of black dust.

'Will your bag never be full, deceitful wretch?' demands Wrnach.

'In the sight of God, it will not, unless a nobleman of Christian blood cometh forward. He must press the food down into the bag using both his feet, and declaring at the same time, 'Enough has now been given'.'

'Is that all?' exclaims the dwarf.
And so he steps forward, pushes a dried boar's head into the bag, and presses it down with both feet, saying, 'Enough has now been given.'

'How right you are, Wrnach Pierce-Thigh,' laughs Kinch, drawing the bag up over the dwarf's head and knotting the strings.

With the bag tied to his saddle, the young victor rides to the nearest village, called Lludd, and asks the villagers to bring their chief to him. They do so, and he gives the bag to the chief, saying 'My name is Lord Kinch. I hereby donate this bag and its contents to the men of Lludd, that they may never know henceforth one minute of rural boredom. Within the bag is a badger. I charge the elders of the village to devise an entirely original game or sport, using my gift.'

And so the elders are summoned and, after three days of deliberation, they devise a game. And on the fourth day they assemble the whole village onto the common to demonstrate the game to their noble visitor. It is explained to Lord Kinch that there are only four rules to the game, namely:
1. *The bag will be hung from a tree.*
2. *Each male villager in turn will strike the bag five times with his foot or staff, asking when he has done so, 'WHAT GAME ARE WE PLAYING?'*

3. *The other male villagers will then reply in unison, 'BADGER IN THE BAG!'*
4. *The game will continue until the badger is dead.*

And thus is acted out,
on a humble village green, with Lord Kinch as witness,
the first ever game of 'Badger In The Bag'.

Mightily pleased with himself, the boy knight departs the village and gallops north, towards the demesne of Tallwch the Hermit. Past the ruin of many a fabulous palace he rides, past lakes and mountains and dark forests, past tall trees aflame and rivers of shining mercury, past exotic beasts with shapes unheard of before or since and wondrous birds soaring by in an ecstasy of song, past cities at war and sweetsmelling farms, past the noble strongholds of Caradawg Stoutarm and Edern son of Gnudd, of Ruthven the Radiant and Peredur Longspear, of Daned son of Oth, Goreu son of Custenhin, and Gobrwy son of Echel the One-eyed.

At length he comes to the Valley of Ysbadden,
where he is greeted by two brindled greyhounds
wearing collars of purple suede. They run beside him,
jumping and darting at each other,
bright-eyed and playful as kittens.
His mare trots on regardless.
On and on.
Trot to canter.
Canter to glide.
And so smooth grows the motion of his steed
that during the last mile of his journey
not a hair of the boy knight's head is disturbed.

Here.

The Hermit lives here.
In this ruined village.
On this dirt street.
In this row of empty halls
and abandoned cottages.

Dismounting, he takes leave of his horse,
follows the evanescence of the hounds
through the absorbing air,
past the first cottage,
feet scuffing dust.

And into the second,
bending head
under lintel.

Into granary,
chapel,
rooms,

feet scuffing dust.

tab: 41

in which the boy knight arrives at his destination
and meets his co-conspirator

'Kinch!'

Marching towards him
through the chalky light
is a thin studentesque figure
in a suit of mustard corduroy.
Soft-bearded, with
cheeks of babbypink,
a bloodless cut of mouth,
an aquiline nose,
waterblue eyes, brow
set in perpetual frown.
Under the left eye, a star tattoo.
Under his arm, a rosewood cane.
Terry Colvyn.

'Good to see you again, old comrade.
Did you leave the package where I said?'
'Yes... well...' replies Kinch, 'There were too many people around to
leave it in the bin, so I hid it behind some bottles in the storeroom.'
'Bottles?'
'Machine solvent.'
'Even better. Good lad. Knew I could trust you.'
'It's a bomb, isn't it?'

'Don't ask, old chap. No, it isn't... well, not exactly. A small incendiary device, as they say. Timed to cause minimum annoyance to the staff.'

'The staff! But you said...'

'I know what I said. But don't worry. Your Mum will be home asleep when the detonator goes off. I made certain of that. Anyway, the alarms will ensure everyone's outside the building within two minutes.'

'What if someone's in the storeroom?'

'Highly improbable. But life's a risky business, and you know what your dad used to say about eggs and omelettes.'

The boy polishes his glasses.

Terry takes him by the shoulder.

'Look, I don't want to be brutal but these are the same bastards that got your father murdered in the prison hospital. Think about it, Kinch – at this very moment they're walking around free as farts and cocky as rats with gold teeth. This is your chance. It's what you want, isn't it?'

'Yes.'

'Good. Now tell me what's been happening since your last visit.'

Kinch tells him everything.

Mad Abel. The dogs. Pigeon. The aunts.

'Any news of Turrentine?'

'No-one knows what he's up to. Pigeon says he's being paid by the Dean to investigate you and your group, but he seems to spend all his time lurking about the Cathedral and the University, so I don't know. Aunt Maeve thinks he's ok.'

'He may or may not be ok, Kinch, but on no account do you let on that you've even so much as heard of me. That could ruin everything.' The grip on his shoulder tightens. 'Understand?'

'You know I won't. Stop it, Terry... you're hurting!'

'Yes, I know you won't. Not deliberately. But talking to a friend, anything can slip out. So never forget who these people are. Every time you see Turrentine remind yourself who's paying him, then picture your dad hung by his feet from the prison ceiling and remember what they did to him. On whose orders, Kinch? Whose orders?'

Hot with anger, the boy twists out of the painful grip. 'Arright... the Dean, the Dean! Stop it will you!'

'I'm sorry, lad. But I've got to be sure,' says Terry, producing a wan smile to accompany the placatory suppressing motion of his hands.

Kinch shrugs and walks to a small south-facing window. 'One more thing about Brownie,' he says, peering out through the dirty glass. 'He's trying to find out about Primrose Jenkins.'

'Is that so? Oh well, much good may it do him. Perhaps he's got his own agenda after all. And who is this guy Pigeon? I never came across him when I was in Axton. What did he say about himself?'

'Nothing much.'

'You sure about that?'

No reply.

'Now listen, Kinch...'

'Alright, alright... he was brought up in the Manse. Used to work at the Cathedral School as a lab assistant. And now he's hiding from the Dean, but I don't know why. That's all.'

With a dampened forefinger, he scrawls the letters 'KW' in a corner of the window and then wipes clean a neat six inch square in its middle.

On the outside of the glass, a dark blurred speck is twitching its way erratically across towards the cleaned patch. Expecting a spider or fly to crawl into the square, Kinch cries out as the black-coated shape of Abel Matthews slips into focus, less than two hundred yards away, scuttling between the stunted trees, drawing closer.
'Terry! It's Abel... he must have followed me!'

'Fuck! Here, grab this.'

Kinch takes the cane of gnarled rosewood thrust at him,
and follows the anarchist through the empty rooms
and out the back door.

tab: 42
which finds Brownie still in bed

Noon.

Half awake.

A stranger. In a strange space...

sky-blue sky, blue-white cloud, stock beech cold varnish hard between cheek and shoulder, firm there, should he be doing this, burntang from the last shot still in the air, wild at a sky-high pigeon and pellet sucked into vacuums beyond the blue and bird down a sideroad hit by the bang before the lead lump reached it, should he be doing this, moving targets the allure of and the always miss and always by mostly miles, keep the bobbled nib in the V of the notched sight and move across clouds tracing outlines of weight and size till the next speck or flapping body, but word gets out and the blue and white stays empty all except that is for a silver pinhead, a plane, a grain of incandescence of invisible fusewire inching its way across the noonday blue, aims and fires, a matter of simple retribution for its some would say cold indifference as the lead lump shuttlecock crashes through fuselage punctures the fuel tank sends plane and pilot plummeting down through the cloudline and through all the strewn vectors from here to empty death as the pinhead continues on its pointless relentless climb wrecking clarity forever it seems

...

...

tab: 43

in which the boy knight's adventures reach a dire conclusion

Noon.
Barley Moor.

Wash of sunlight.
Heath of grey furze.
Two figures, jogging,
every few seconds
looking back, back
at the wasted hamlet.
'There!' Kinch gasps.

In the doorway of the cottage,
a black bloated polyp. Through
the glare and the emptiness,
a tracheitic roar.

Terry takes the boy's arm and hurries him through a swathe of low gorse
to the edge of what appears to be an abandoned building site. Heaps of
unused brick submerged by moss and grass. A half-buried generator,
attended by the rotting jetsam of all the building trades – wheelbarrows,
trestles, spades, cable spools, pickaxes. 'Jesuit seminary,' he mutters. 'Or
that was the plan, before the MoD stole the land.' The only finished piece
of construction is a rectangular concrete pit with shutter-boarded walls.
In the centre stands a lone pillar, streaked with rills of orange oxide
dribbling down from its iron reinforcing rods. They crouch low, behind

the generator. 'Push him over the edge, that's our best bet,' says Terry, looking round. 'No-one ever comes here. He'll starve to death if the fall doesn't...'

Another roar. Too close.

They see it through the ribs of the generator.

The creature. Closing.

Terry finds a shovel. Tests it on a rock.

The blade breaks off in a puff of dust.

Seventy yards away.

Kinch tightens his grip on the rosewood cane.
The wiry anarchist searches for a heavier weapon,
his fingertips drumming intermittently
on the stock of a belted sheath knife.

Fifty.

The boy points to the arc of a rusty pick-axe blade protruding from a tangle of dead grass and bracken. Terry pulls it from the undergrowth, grips it by the point and swings it around at waist height. 'We'll separate. I'll keep him busy. You see if you can trip him.'

Ten.

The eyes of the gatekeeper
squint out through wet flesh
at his puny opposition –
a scrawny fluff-bearded weirdo

with a pickblade he can hardly lift
and a crazy little runt with a walking stick.
A black carcoat hangs over Abel's belly.
His nipples are sore from the rough cloth.
Sweat trickles and tickles down his cleavage.
The buckle at the waist of his bermuda shorts digs like a fork into his
gut. He reaches down with his left hand to lift his belly and move the
buckle to a new position. In his right hand dangles a wooden club,
spiked with nails.
He stands for a while,
angry, but in no rush,
feet spread wide apart,
inviting air into his shorts,
onto his burning scrotum.
Angry. Angry at his body.
Angry at this evil snotnose brat
who's killed both his beautiful dogs.
Him first. The weirdo can wait.
A hand rises to remove from his damp skull a greasy denim sailing cap
which with a deft flick he sends frisbeeing towards the boy, who ducks
and throws it back.
The weirdo says something to the runt.
They separate.

Abel snorts.
Starts his run.
The ground shakes.
This is more like it.
What he was made for.

The running feels good,
sends blood fizzing round his body.
He grips the club with both hands.

Kinch turns to run, startled by the fat creature's speed.
The gap closes. He runs faster,
keeping to the edge of the pit.
But not fast enough.

At the blurred margin of his field of vision
Abel glimpses a sudden movement
from the man in yellow corduroy –
and howls in astonishment as pain convulses his left shoulder.
Twisting round, he sees the brass-ringed handle of a sheath knife
projecting from his back like a freak limb.
He stops. Lets his club fall to ground.
Tries to pull out the knife, but can't reach.
Picks up his club, turns to face the challenge.
'Come and get it... f-f-faggotfucker.'

The anarchist advances,
wielding his makeshift weapon like a reaper's scythe.
Abel shuffles forward along the side of the pit to meet him,
trying to ignore the pain in his shoulder. 'Come, cunt,' he spits.
As they close, Terry starts swinging the pickblade around himself,
slowly at first but pivoting faster and faster,
round and round on a point just inches
from the mouth of the concrete basin.

Abel keeps going,
pain under control,
head a humming dynamo.
When the bearded dervish is close
and the spike is fanning the skin of his belly,
he lifts his club into the path of the whirling metal.

The impact leaves him unshaken,
standing legs apart like a small mountain.
On Terry, the effect is somewhat different.
As his weapon strikes the gatekeeper's club, the recoil rips the blade
out of his hands and sends it spinning into the air, where it hovers
high above him in slow-motion mockery until at last the spade-end
flashes down and cracks him on the temple. The world and his fat
foe dance before him. One foot stands on nothing, lowers into
nothing. Capsize... capsize... now an arm, now a shoulder is grabbed,
grappled, gripped by a soft stinking vice which hauls him back onto
solid ground. But then the vice drops to his ribs, lifts him up high,
higher, his feet kicking wind.
A hard knot of knuckle grinds into his lower back.
The sweating crown of the brute's head forces up his chin.
'Take the knife out!' wheezes Abel. The vice relaxes,
allowing Terry to reach behind the massive shoulder
and grasp the roughened leather of the handle.
'Fucking pull it out, you cunt!'
The blade seems jammed in bone.
He works it back and round and
round and down before it finally slips out.
The vice tightens.

'Now fucking DROP it!'
The knife drops,
clatters to the pit floor.
Tighter. No breath. Still tighter.
Can't breathe, can't...
He hears a rib crack,
and then another.
The last thing...
the last thing he sees
is blood from his mouth
splashing in petals onto the skull beneath,
spreading like squirts of red syrup on a wetted ball
of baskin-robbins clotted cream   vanilla.

Kinch.
...*daisy*...
...*dandelion*...
...*daisy*...*poppy*...
...*dandelion*...*daisy*...
...*harebell*...*poppy*...*daisy*...
'...forget-me-not,' says Kinch,
skirting the pit, balancing along
the cracked lip of grey concrete,
using outcrops of weeds and wildflowers
as distraction from the impending horror.
'...forget-me-not, forget-me-not,' says he,
as the frail blue membranes are crushed
by a quick twist of his steel-tipped cane.

Looks up at the bloated two-legged daymare
swaying before him.
Abel-Terry. Love-in-Death.

Another rib snaps as the gatekeeper adjusts his embrace.
Face delta'd with victim goo, eyes clogged, mouth stretched to a wide
grin, the creature seems to have forgotten all about Kinch. The boy
stares in disbelief. Terry's head has fallen back, the neck apparently
broken. The only sound is a corrosive wheezing from the huge chest.
Running lightly around behind the pair, Kinch takes hold of the tipped
end of his rosewood cane and aims a blow at the back of Abel's head.
The buboed handle connects just below target,
between skull and coatcollar,
jarring the axis vertebra
into the lower brainstem.
'GHUGHHH!'
At first Abel stands firm,
his lifeless burden clutched to his chest.
But wheeze turns to gurgle. Legs crumple.
He topples sideways, over the edge, out of sight.
Kinch hears the thud, walks to the pit, and peers over the rim.
Terry's body must have cushioned his fall, for the gatekeeper is already
on his feet, wiping the blood from his eyes, staggering from wall to wall
and collapsing onto his hands and knees when he realises there's no way
out. A fit of asthmatic coughing pummels his ribs. He retches and spits
foam for minutes on end, crawling round his dungeon like a beetle in a
matchbox, looking for tools, weapons, anything, leaving behind him a
trail of smeared blood from the wounded shoulder. He sees something
shiny sticking out from under the anarchist's jacket.

He grunts. Takes the dead man's knife.
Lifts himself. Straightens.
Tries to throw it at the boy. Left-handed.
Pain backfires in his shoulder.
The arm drops to his side, useless.
Kinch picks up a stone. Throws it.
Collects a handful.
Smooth pebbles, lumps of concrete.
Aims them one by one.
The third hits the target.
And the fourth. Too easy.
He collects more and aims them at the bloody skull.
Abel stops moving, allowing the stones to hit him where they will.
A broken whistling noise seeps out, a sound like 'help me', repeated
over and over. A wedge of concrete ricochets off the back of his head,
causing fresh blood to stream down the temple and off the end of his
nose. The body shakes with a quiet sobbing.
Kinch drops the stones and turns to leave.
Seeing Abel's cap on the grass,
he skims it down into the pit,
to hoopla the head. Misses.

Fifty yards away, the screams start,
and continue for a while, but
fainter, fainter, fainter,
just echoes, birdcries,
on a distant wind.

tab: 44

in which a paid informer finds a new vocation

Noon.
The edge of Farmtown.
An untended field, a pond.
The grasshopper trembles, or the page trembles, in the breeze.
Brownie extends an emaciated finger. When his fingertip touches the dry stalk of the nearest jumping leg, nothing happens. He tries again, this time pushing the leg sideways a little. As the insect takes off, he feels the recoil through the thickness of his notebook, and imagines it springing from the palm of his hand.

Opening stanza. Fifth draft.
May never leaves you,
    abba..................,
        entr..................,
            etc...   etc...

Scratches out everything apart from the first line, first word, then that, then why o why this same old blundering bloody splitskid down the same old airless helix-vortex till here he is again peeper-deep up his own winkerstinker and none the same old fucking wiser.
Turns back the pages.
Re-lives all the other
bad beginnings.

And yet...

The breeze fans his cheek, rustles reeds in the muddy pond.
A deadskin veil of cloud, high diffuser of the light, thins out.
On the opposite bank, a farmer's windpump creaks into life.
He turns the book over.

The air tastes sweet.
A rosebay willow herb
leans its head on his shoulder.
He breaks off a spear of wild barley
and harpoons a dock leaf.
His boulder seat grows uncomfortable.
He shifts a little. Disturbs a moth.
Another movement, small, clockwork,
on the ground near his right shoe.
Pulse of a toad's throat. He looks.
Tracks with the light in the light's elucidation
of the damp-and-olive bump-and-hollow flesh.
Re-opens the notebook, and starts to copy with his micro-rollerball pen
the shape and shading of the toad's head, and as he copies he starts to feel
in his own reptile bones the weight of each dark form. Pen to scriber to
scalpel, to spatula, spike, tentacle-antenna, dissecting, reconstructing.

Before the drawing is finished, the toad
staggers off into the undergrowth.
He shuts the book.
Walks back to Axton.
In a spun hub
              of love.

tab: 45

which accompanies Pigeon and Kaisa on their first rendezvous

Noon.

The City Museum.

Gallery X1V: *MACEDONIA*.

'I shall call you Piet.'

'Pigeon's ok. I don't mind.'

'Yes, I know. But Piet's... '

'...more respectable?'

'Maybe. But you'll have to put up with it. Unless of course you've a better suggestion.'

'Oh no, that's fine,' he grins. 'Take a bit of getting used to, that's all. Kaisa, on the other hand, is a good name. It suits you.'

'Oh?'

'You know... soft and hard. Well... mostly hard actually...'

She throws back her head and gives such a squeal of raucous laughter that an entire squadron of blue-faced Bible students with vermilion 'Bible Tour' badges stapled to the communal upper thorax turns around in disapproval.

'You make me sound like a box of chocolates!'

'No comment.'

'How's the arm?'

She touches the bandage,

her fingers short, walnut-dark.

'Much better, thanks.'

Encircling the room, along an eye-level frieze of end-to-end marble tablets, shuffles an unruly cavalcade. Satyrs promenade with boars and goats. Horses with sphinxes. Hounds with hens. A faceless lion sinks its teeth into the back of a fallen hind. A bearded long-eared man crawls over the ground clutching a herald's caduceus.

Centre floor. A tomb. A box of battered limestone, carved on each side with whimsical episodes extracted from the legendpool of an obscure Macedonian cult. Kaisa chuckles, pointing to one undamaged corner. A lumpish harpy with a tiny long-robed man in her arms hovers over a grieving woman. The harpy's nipples are erect, pushing into the man's abdomen as he fondly strokes her chin.

'Coffee?' asks Pigeon.
'Sounds good. But I've not much time.'

Their unequal shapes refracted by crystal,
their footsteps echoing off the high walls,
they walk the precincts of Archaic Greece,
lingering over red-figured kraters,
pointy-bottomed amphorae,
amulets of hammered gold,
brooches of blackened silver,
and gawping at the great broken lions
from the Sanctuary of Apollo at Didyma.

An attendant talks in tongues.
The Bible students make notes.

Down a twist of stairs, and
into the small basement cafe.
Empty. Just opened.
Coffee times-two from the serving hatch.
On the till, a big stately black woman.
'Tank you kindly, my deeeer,' she smiles
with a special look for Pigeon.

They settle at a corner table.
Kaisa answers his questions.
'I grew up in Finland – a village near Tampere. Just Mother and me and
my two sisters. Left school early to make ends meet. In shopwork till my
sisters found husbands, then back to school, then nursing college. Then
Mother died and I moved here. Married. Divorced. There you have it.'
'Any children?'
'The marriage didn't last six months, though of course there has been
the occasional man, but I've always... No. No children.'
Something attracts her attention on the other side of the room.
'What happened to the marriage? If you don't mind...'
'Friends tried to warn me and I suppose I should have known better,
but after eight hard years of work and study, I was just about ripe for
the picking-and-sniffing-and-taking-and-being-dropped-in-the-dirt
by the first moderately goodlooking simian to flex his hairy pectorales
in my general direction.   But... no harm done, I suppose.'
'He still around?'
'Not likely. First hint of insubordination from yours truly and off he
went. Sucked into the wide open vacuities of Australasia, so I hear.
Or so I like to believe.'

The Bible students arrive and arrange themselves on the opposite side of the tiny café, as far away as possible but still taking up more than half the available space. A youth with thick spectacles and a bow tie is propounding *sotto voce* to his fellow pietists on the First Cause argument for a Creative Deity.

Kaisa's mouth crimps disapprovingly. She turns to look at the only other customer. Waiting at the hatch is a plump fortyish woman bloused in violet and wrapped in a thick skirt of bumble-bee tartan secured at the front by a giant safety pin. Her big straw curls are topped by an outsize tam-o'-shanter of frazzled lemon mohair. Her smooth cheeks are rouged beyond red. The woman seems embarrassed by her appearance and hurries past them carrying a trayload of English breakfast to a table in the only unoccupied corner, a shadowed place, half-hidden by a mosaic pillar.

She leans closer to him.
'That's Letty. Used to be married to the bursar of Augustine College, a real swine. She divorced him for mental cruelty but was drinking so heavily throughout the whole lousy business, as well as having an affair with one of the dons – Harold Admetus, you've probably heard of him – that she lost custody of her three children. In and out of institutions ever since. Admetus dropped her straightaway, of course. I treated her once, a long time ago now. But it's good to see her. In those days she never left the house.'
'She's often here,' Pigeon murmurs, elbows on table, chin on palms, rocking to and fro, drawn imperceptibly forward. Kaisa sips her coffee. He feels a wave of her hair touch and move gently against his own crop of dry white wisps. Chocolate. Chocolate on her breath.

He lifts his eyes, to see hers looking hard at him,
through him, with a kind of blind ferocity.
He backs away. Asks a polite question.
Skin tightens round poolblue fires. 'What schoolwork?' she laughs,
and tells him tales of capers, pranks, feral truant wanderings among
the wooded lakes of Finland. He has a question ready for every pause,
watching her face for every smallest turn and tic and transformation.

1.05 p.m. Letty and the students are long gone.
More customers arrive. Office workers, in for lunch.
She glances up at the clock. The second half of her split shift starts soon.
'Tell you what. Why don't you come round to my place this Friday and
I'll cook you dinner. You'd better not refuse because I hate cooking and
its not an offer I make every day, so... Great honour, you see.'
'Thanks very much, Kaisa. If you're sure.'
'Dare hesitate and I'll never speak to you again.'
'Then in that case...'
'Good. That's settled. Eight o'clock, Friday. It's the last house at the
top of Deacon Drive. Near Maeve and Stevie's road. The ground
floor flat with the yellow door. You can't miss it.'

'Yellow door. Eight o'clock. Thanks... I'll look forward to it.'

'Bye, Piet.'

'Bye... '

tab: 46

in which a plot is hatched

'.....SKKTCHKKTTCH...TCHTTTKKCHK...SSKTKKESSSSSSSSSCRITCH SCRITCH SCRATCHIN AT THE DEVIL'S DOOR SSSS KEKETCHE SSSSKETCHE SSSSKETCHE SSSSKETCHE DRIBBY DIB DABBIN AT THE BLOODRUN JAW SSSSKETCHE SSSSKETCHE SSSSKETCHE DRIPPY DRIP DROPPIN ON THE DEVIL'S FLOOR SSSSKETCHE SSSSKETCHE SSSSKETCHE SSSSKETCHE....'

1.55 p.m.

Two cherry-red ball speakers rattle over the lunchtime clientele of Carsons Café. Posters on the walls announce that rehearsals for a new musical at next door's Criterion Theatre are under way. In a window overlooking the street, with their backs turned to the bedlam of bit-actors, musicians and stage hands, two tall figures on barstools cradle empty-but-still-warm american-style coffee mugs in their hands. Brownie, taller by an arched little finger, does most of the talking. On the table is a sheet of pencilled diagrams which he erases or amends at the prompting of his companion. 'How's that?' he asks. 'If we need more help I can probably rope in a couple of friends.'

'No. Fewer the better. I'll set up the projector on my own. That'll be fine.' The second man, with a square, cautious face, is BeJay, a.k.a. Bart or 'Barmy' Jessop, an ex-crony of Terry Colvyn who had once caroused and polemicized his way through Actor's School alongside Brownie and the now-defunct anarchist, but who in the end opted for the metered life and a settled career as Managing Director of the Criterion, Axton's only theatre.

'What about sockets?'

'I've checked,' replies Brownie. 'Oh, and will it be ok to borrow a roll of linen from props for the dropscreen? It'll just need fixing to a couple of battens. Or would the wall itself be good enough?'

'It certainly would. But first give me that memory stick you nicked from Admetus and I'll get it copied. See you here later then. Four o'clock?'

'Thanks, BeJay.'

'My pleasure old man. Be great to nail the bastard.'

As they weave their way through the boisterous company to the open door, the lyrics of the rebel's dirge die away once again.

'.....SSSSKETCHE SSSSKETCHE SSSSKETCHESCRITCH SCRITCH SCRATCHIN OF A DEAD RED CLAW SSSSKETCHE SSSSKETCHE SSSSKETCHE CLIPPY CLIP CLOPPIN OF HIS HOOVES NO MORE SSSSKETCHE SSSSKETCHE SSSSKETCHE CRY CRY CRYIN OUTSIDE THE LAW.....'

tab: 47

in which Pigeon learns of the events on Barley Moor
and makes a phone call

'Kinch?'
Out of blackness.
'Kinch?'
Out of blackness.
Light.
Lucifer.
Red heart of it.
'Kinch?'
Fingers meshed in wire.
Out of blackness.
'Kinch?'

'Kinch?'

The boy looks up.
But sees only the steel door thrown open
by a madness edged with spitting gold,
the flailing two-armed beacon of a man on fire.
It comes straight at him. Through the wire.
Foliate black hands cover his own,
the demon mask only inches away.
Hair and flesh aflame.
Through the wire.

Pigeon and Maeve stay by his bed.

One hour of nightmare. One hour of sleep.

At last he sits up, pale and drained, body rigid.

5.30 p.m. Maeve slips downstairs.

'You awake, Kinch?'

'Yes.'

'Where d'you go?'

'The factory. Gridmore's dead.'

As the boy's story unfolds

Pigeon feels the bedroom shrink,

feels a grim wind chilling his blood.

'Alright,' he says, his eyes blurring, birthmark twitchy. 'I'll phone the Dean now, if that's what you want. He can tell the police and get a search party set up for the morning.'

'Thanks... '

Maeve re-enters with a suppertray of boiled egg in an eggcup, toast soldiers and a mug of tea. By the time she reaches the bed, Kinch has dropped back into a deep sleep. After a few words with her, Pigeon creeps downstairs, gives the tray to Stevie, and asks for the phone.

He picks up the handset.

And dials,

reaching in his pocket

for the jade monkey.

'Is that the Dean? It's Pigeon... I'm calling about Abel... He's badly injured at the bottom of a pit on the other side of Barley Moor... Can't say... Yes, I'm sure. So, you'll see to it?'

Pigeon winces, then scowls.
'You want to see me tonight? Both of you? Very well.'

He replaces the phone, eats Kinch's supper,
pulls on a fusty overcoat that
Stevie has looked out for him,
and departs,

just as the grandfather clock
is limbering crankily up
to strike nine.

tab: 48

One hour later,
he is still walking, very slowly,
in the lopsided dawdle that earned him his name all those years ago. The
Blood Wall obliterates sky and stars and moon. Under the arch of the
West Barbican he rests on a bench of slabbed granite.
Cold through corduroy.
Cobbles at his feet.
Marble at his back.
Past shut. Future shut.
Orphan driftwood out of nowhere, going nowhere.
Dollop of discoloured scum in an Axton gutter.
'Come on,' he croaks.
It'll pass. It always does.

From the Barbican the road slopes down towards the river, then up
and over Sad Butchers (originally 'Bitches') Bridge, a favoured suicide
spot during Axton's and everywhere else's febrile golden age of
jewbaiting witchhunting Christian rectitude. The last streetlight is
an ironwrought three-branch candelabra affair of chains and leaves
and dolphins, erected on the last apex of the bridge wall.

He climbs onto the wall, grips a cold fishtail
and leans out over the water.
Daring himself. Knowing he won't.
The river swirls with newfound gusto.

Heavy rainfall, from the hills.
Flecks of yellow glint and splinter,
mirrored on mamba.

Oh, Kaisa!
Swings out. Pulls back.
Jumps lightly from wall to ground.
Til tomorrow, stupid.
Til tomorrow.
Easy.

Away from the bridge the pavement narrows and gives way to grass
verge. The grass is wet so he walks on the road. Huge oaks to his left
hide the moon, his way lit only and dimly by the feckless drizzle of the
stars. He ransacks field and hedgerow for tremors of hue, glimmer of
detail. Greys come to blues and dusty greens. Shapes flow into new
shapes. The starbeds tilt. Left-right-left twists the tarmac ribbon. He is
halfway to the Manse before any traffic passes, and even then nothing
more than the chug-chug-rattle of his old Latin teacher's moped.
Recognising the deerstalkered profile on its way to assist with pre-
matins cleaning duties at the Cathedral, he jumps onto the verge, backs
into wetness. The rider seems to hear and slows to a crawl, scanning
gloom but seeing nothing. Once the moped has gone, Pigeon moves off
himself, chilled through, trouser-bottoms slapping ankles, the borrowed
coat damp with dewfall. In a panic to ward off a headcold before he sees
Kaisa tomorrow, he starts trotting, skipping and galloping along until
his blood runs hot. Stopping, he wipes the sweat from his brow, catches
his breath, and then resumes the journey in alternate bouts of jogging
and walking.

His clothes feel wet, but he doesn't mind. A nail works its way up through the heel of his shoe, but he doesn't mind. A car, the first car, comes dinning towards him, headlights raging, forcing him up the steep bank. Mud scratches his hands. But he doesn't mind.
He strides along the tufted camelback ridge,
re- and re-living the strangeness,
the ninety minutes in the museum.

Here, already. Stop.
The Gates.
Stop.
One pillar a ruin.
The other, the nearest, complete.
A square column, stepped cornice, sphere of pitted limestone.
To the right and level with the stone ball hangs the moon. Pillar and moon are the same cold stuff, secreting an alchemic bleach onto thicket and wall and rutted land. He slithers down the bank and walks through the gate into the drive. Hurries past the massive trees. Looks in spite of himself, and sees, between the trunks, the eyeless skull of Abel's house. The half-doors to the ramshackle stables which once held the two mastiffs are gaping wide.

Spooked by the crackling granite underfoot,
he steps sideways onto the sward of the Water Meadow.
The lights of the Manse sail out from behind a copse of poplars.
A sudden noise causes him to swivel round
and drop to his knees.
Them.

Horsehooves and phaeton-wheels rip through the gravel, pass him by. Clarissa overhangs the horses like a brick Boudicca, eyes fixed ahead, reins dangling from the arthritic wrist. He glimpses the Dean pressed back against seat and handrail. The carriage shrinks into silence, turns, disappears into the courtyard.

He waits a few minutes,
and follows.

tab: 49

in which Pigeon confronts his inheritance

10.30 p.m.
The jade feels
warm, sticky.

> *Something landed on the floor.*
> *It was his son's head! Holding it in his hands,*
> *the old man wept and cried out 'My boy is done for!'*

The Library. Inside.
Caught. In memory's web.
He looks about him. Becomes again
that captive child whose only contact with other children was the
sound of Clarissa and the fledgeling Dean playing in some distant
ante-room many walls hence, whose only companions were the bored
pestle-faced tutors, probably underpaid and certainly unfit for any
real job in any real school. Above the oak-panelled dado, patches of
elizabethan distemper still cling doggedly to the deeper hollows of the
rough stonework. He remembers picking off big flakes of it, waiting.
Desk no longer there.

> *Moments later a foot dropped from the skies.*
> *Then more limbs fell down this way and that,*
> *until his son was scattered all over the square.*
> *In great sadness, Liu Ch'o picked up the pieces,*
> *placing them gently...*

The door opens. In walks the Dean, followed by Clarissa. They seat themselves at either end of a big leather chesterfield, one of several pieces of tired but agreeable furniture strewn around this bookshelved half of the long chamber. He sits facing them across an inky table, in a formal carving chair that puts his own eye-level a good six inches above theirs. 'Time for a few facts, I think,' begins the Dean, glancing at Clarissa, who nods, not taking her eyes off Pigeon. 'You've probably guessed as much, but you are Clarissa's half-brother. Mother to you both was Prudence Jenkins, the blind street musician and pauper-philanthropist cum all-round virtuous lady whose statue you have no doubt admired in Cathedral Square. Famous in her own lifetime as a do-gooder, but rumoured even then to have fallen into unwholesome company, she was, as we now know thanks to my man Creech, nothing more and nothing less than a streetwalker turned pimp turned gang-leader, and, in the end, turned highly successful racketeer. She bought the Manse from the bankrupt Blunderston family at a knock-down price, mainly we think out of vanity, but also as a place to keep her children and possibly her lovers as they came and went. She seems to have spawned at least five children by various men, all given rather whimsical surnames, all brought up in ignorance of each other, with only Clarissa and your good self surviving into adolescence. Clarissa was the only normal healthy one of the whole brood. As for myself and my own parentage, we're not so sure. I recollect being brought here when I was about six, but nothing before that. The most plausible theory is that I'm the unregistered bastard of Lizzie Holmes, your mother's guide and lieutenant. But I was, nevertheless, treated by the old lady herself as if I'd been her real son, on equal terms with Clarissa, unlike you.'

Ca2(Mg,Fe)5Si8O22(OH)2
Calcium Magnesium Iron Silicate Hydroxide
Crystal system – monoclinic, in a fibrous compact mass

The desiccated cleric relaxes into the chesterfield. 'According to the older servants here, from the very first your mother wanted nothing to do with you, mainly because of your birthmark. The devil's blight she called it. She was also convinced you were a half-wit, one of her lovers at the time being a circus strongman, handsome by all accounts but a notorious loon. So. You will at least be comforted by the news that we are probably not related, you and I. However, and be that as it may, none of our births were registered so none of us really knows the identity of his or her father.' Closing his eyes, he brings his fingertips together in order to screen his face. 'Thanks to your unsavoury peeping tom activities, you now know that Clarissa and I are, so to speak, an item. We have been for some time, and will remain so for many years to come. But that's our business. What you need to be told is that in her will your mother left everything to your half-sister and myself, with no provision for you apart from board, lodging, and some fairly basic private education.

Lustre – vitreous
Cleavage – inapplicable
Other characteristics – very tough, stronger than steel

'So this is where we are. Despite your sly behaviour and your ridiculous running off as though you were being kept prisoner, we still feel under some obligation to you. As you can clearly manage outside our supervision, we've decided to give you a reasonably adequate monthly allowance which will continue until you try to interfere again in our affairs. Here are the details of the bank accounts we've opened for you. Personally, I'm happy never to see you again. Clarissa, however, against my advice, insists she is going to... well...' The big woman lowers her head and smoothes her dress over her thighs. The Dean leans forward and places on the table a thick envelope stamped with the blue logo of Axton's municipal bank.

With a smile on his face and the picture of an idiot leopard-skinned strongman father taking shape in his mind, Pigeon reaches across, and rips the envelope in half. Puts the halves together and rips again.
'No mother,' he says.
Walks towards Clarissa.
And rips again.
The torn squares drop into her lap.
'No sister.'
He turns to leave and starts walking.
From across the room the Dean gives a barely audible squeak and bounds forward like a hungry gibbon, catapulting himself through the air, crashing into Pigeon's upper back.
Arms clamp round neck, legs round waist.
Teeth sink into tough neck muscle.

But Clarissa is there.
She takes her beloved
by his tailored collar,
drags him off, and hurls him
spinning across the polished floor.
Pigeon says nothing. Continues
as if nothing has happened.

She watches, flushed, tears welling,
as her half-brother lumbers out of the room.

tab: 50

On his way back through Farmtown to the aunts' cottage, Pigeon makes a detour through Walsingham Gardens, an oval park enclosed by half a dozen poplars and a neatly trimmed hedge of spotted laurel. Clear-headed but worn out from his night of walking, he rests on a long wooden bench.

Around him are young rowans and copper beeches, newly planted courtesy of the Abbey Guild, or so brags a shiny brass plate welded onto one of the spiked cages shielding some of the smaller trees from the pubescent ministrations of the Farmtown buckaroos. In the park's centre, five circular rosebeds surround a deactivated drinking fountain.

6.00 a.m.
He leans back. Lets the poison dribble out. Feet, calves, thighs, stomach. Hands, arms, shoulders, neck. Tendrils break through the skin of his back, take root in the grain of the oak slats.
The sky is cloudless, the air clean.
He breathes deep. On his eyelids
a bliss of warm sunlight displaces
the shadow from the poplars.
Hands caress rough wood.
Head drops back, softly,
onto rough wood.

One hour later, pain surges across the back of his head and neck. He blinks at the sun. Stretches. Rolls to one side, and then the other, teasing out the aches from his body. He sits forward, elbows on knees, fingertips kneading suppleness into his neck, dislodging crumbs of dried blood from the Dean's bite. He looks round at the park. Several of the outer benches have been claimed by solitary males like himself. A thin man in a dark unkempt suit, scarecrow hair and crooked half-spectacles is visiting each one in turn, asking a question, and then moving on to the next. Pigeon rummages in the pockets of his coat for loose change.

But. No beggar. Over the spectacle rims, myopic loris eyes.
'I'm looking for Turrentine. Do you know where he is, please?'
Syllable-meticulous. Something... familiar...
'You mean Brownie Turrentine?'
'Yes. Where would I find him, please?'
'No idea. Can I give him a message?'
'No... at least...'

A movement. Through the trees.
Two figures in green overalls approach along the gravel path. The man catches sight of them, turns to go, seems undecided, then sits down beside Pigeon, gripping his arm. 'Tell him... it's Drench. Drench is Green George. The one who does it.'
'Does what?' asks Pigeon.

The men in overalls arrive. 'Stop bothering people, James,' instructs the first. 'Come with us now. Your mother's asking for you.' Meekly, the dejected creature allows himself to be led away.
'Does what?' Pigeon yells after him.

The minders look back
with an unpleasant smirk,
a shrug of resignation.

Only when they are out of sight
does it come to him. Creech.
The Dean's accountant.

For one more hour
he stays in the park,
on his bench,
with the trees,
                with the roses,
                        and the dead drinking fountain.

tab: 51

in which Kinch is disabused by his mother
of a crucial misapprehension

11.00 a.m.
From his berth,
he sees tiny jets of smoke
squirting through the tannoy.
Voices creak out across the blazing ship.
'Are you there? Are you there, Captain?...
Breakfast on the bridge sir, when you're ready...'

Fire burns a hole in the ceiling and the hole drags its molten edge to the
top of the cabin walls. Curls of smouldering paper drift down and settle
on his face. He wipes away the soft black dust.

'Kinch?'
His mother. Looking down at him. She sits him up and feeds him puffed
wheat like a baby, while around him the smoke and flames of his gutted
cruiser give way to the simple seagreen shapes of his own room.

Home. Back home.
He flinches, diverting a spoonful of milky cereal onto the pillow.
'Shouldn't be here,' he chokes. 'The Dean's after me...'
She takes his wrists.
'No, Kinch. Listen to me. You've got it wrong.
Terry lied. I know he was a friend of your Dad's, but he lied.'
The milk tastes sour.

'I saw your father in the prison hospital, on his last day, in his own room. The staff treated him well, so he said. Of course he died there, but it was cancer, not politics and certainly not torture, that finished him off.'
The fingers loosen around his wrists
but the eyes draw him in.
He turns away.

'Terry lied, Kinch. He was using you. Like your Dad, just the same. Anyway, I've spoken to the Dean. They think you were responsible in some way for the fire at Gridmore's factory and the death of the manager. I don't understand, but he's promised not to press charges, so long as you go back to school and stop pestering him.'

He blinks hair from his eyes, feels for his glasses.
Darkness. In the sea below, dozens of oil-covered survivors cling to anything that floats. A few wave up at him, unaware of the noose of flame closing in on them by the second.

The fingers tighten.

'Did you hear what I said, Kinch?'
'Yes. Everything's fine.'
'Look at me. There's something else. About your father...'
She points at, then touches, a faded scar on her forehead, a pale crescent running parallel with her left eyebrow. 'This wasn't done in a cycling accident like I always say. He did it. Your brave father. Soon after we were married. Threw me across the kitchen into a glass door.' She pulls down the high collar of her blouse. Another scar, fresher, zigzags diagonally from below the ear to the middle of the windpipe.

'And this one too. A broken beer-bottle. Wasn't drunk. Nor even angry.
Just in the mood.'

Layers of dead bark fall from his face.
He locates his glasses, polishes the lens
on his pyjama sleeve, rubbing hard, slow.
His mother lays a hand on his, until he stops.
'I should have told you before.
I never dreamt...'

The oil spillage has burnt itself out.
Nothing left now. Nothing but
a few lumps of floating charcoal
on the ruffled swell of the ocean.

tab: 52

6.00 p.m.
Underground.
Level: Minus 2.
Storage and Parlour.

Student Forty-nine,
a late arrival, shivers
as the rubber doors
slap together.

The Storage Room is a narrow oblong cellar. Along each side, in a
motorised articulated shelving system, stretches a row of closely packed
two-tier bunk units, all occupied. The sole means of support for each
seven foot board and its tenant is a single tubular bracket, thick as a
scaffold pole, projecting from a network of steel-rimmed channels cut
into the white enamel of the storeroom wall. Each bracket has its own
vertical track rising to a junction with one of two horizontal supertracks.
The upper row of bunks is waist high, leaving only a tight clearance to
the bodies below. At the far end of the room a dozen diminutive maids
scuttle among the bunks enacting well-oiled rites of barbery, ablution,
and sterilization upon their unconscious subjects.

The tutor group processes down the broad centre aisle. Halfway along,
at a gesture from their professor, they stop to deploy themselves neatly
around one of the unserviced bunk units.

'New admissions, 307 and 308. Brother and sister, twins, highly unusual. The janitor's offering odds on which'll survive longer. My money's on the female, artificially rendered following a suicide attempt, with a history of benign ovarian tumours but otherwise healthy. Sixty-eight. Older than most.'

Green George rolls back the bedsheet to reveal a delicate body of refulgent whiteness. Breasts cling to the ribcage like strips of baconfat. Beneath the right dug, wedged between arm and thorax is the full brown bladder of a colostomy bag. He bends lower, forward, over the torso. Latex fingers prise open the jaw, peel back the lips. 'No teeth, you see. She won't be needing them anymore. Decay leads to mouth infection, so we pull them out. The healthy ones are pulverised and recycled, recycled as... Guess what, anyone?'
'Toothpaste, sir?' ventures Five.
'An appealing idea, my son. But no. Laboratory-grade platinum polish, in point of fact...' He shines a torch into the open maw. 'Perfect. Special care has to be taken against sores developing in the redundant mouth as antibiotics leave the subject unproductive for a good ten days. Blood must be clean, above all else. Hygiene, remember, has always been the second principal of sustainable zootechnics. And the first, numero Seven, is what?'
Seven takes a breath. 'Mechanisation, sir?'
'Well done,' smiles the surgeon, in a good mood, apparently.

The worried gaze of student Forty-nine has wandered to a unit at the far end of the room, where four maids are working. Two are kneeling, busy with the lower bunk. The other two have finished, and are turning away from their naked client. A red light on the wall above them begins to flash. All four bustle into the centre aisle, clutching bedsheets. From under each bunkboard, a pair of short metal guardrails flips out and up, alongside the bare arms. Three loud beeps, and the whole unit motors steadily upward. At ten feet, another unit close by starts to rise. At fifteen feet, the coupled bunks jerk to a stop and move off again at right angles, horizontally, toward the tutor group, along the elevated tramlines. Machinery behind the wall ticks and whinnies, but the bunks run smoothly. Green George beams at the dismay on the face of his least enthusiastic student. 'Impressive, n'est-ce pas, Forty-nine? A few glitches to be sorted out, but this is the model for ten more processing plants, under construction as I speak.'

The migrating bunks are overhead. Forty-nine strains back his neck to see them, gulping bile as he does so. His adam's apple pistons up and down in its badly shaved throat. The surgeon can't resist. With a long muscular finger he flicks the energetic protuberance hard on its nose, and then sweeps out a long leg to kick the unhappy student's feet from under him. A noise of gears crunching escapes from Forty-nine's hapless gullet, as its proprietor writhes on the floor between the bunks. 'Up, insect!'
The insect struggles to its feet, spluttering, shaking its head.
'Buck your ideas up, sunshine, or you'll be back here toutey-suitey. Comme vache. Comprenez?'
'Yes sir. Sorry sir.'

The surgeon motions Thirty-five to replace Tinkerbelle's bedsheet, and orders Thirty-six and Thirty-seven to examine her brother below. That done, he leads his class out of the room and back into the corridor. Left, and briskly left again. Through a door labelled '*MILKING PARLOUR*'.

The pair of bunk units from Storage have separated and are already in place on opposite sides of the tiled white chamber. From a needle in the left forearm of each naked subject a coil of suspended nylon tubing leads to one of four dustbin-size glass drums, which are in turn connected by rubber-sheathed hoses to the central pump, an intricately built engine of polished brass and stainless steel. Five orange-smocked orderlies are in attendance, one per bunk and one to check the gauges attached at intervals to hoses and machinery.

The surgeon lines up his students against the wall.
Stipulates. Unnecessarily. Silence. Attention.

Columns of dark blood twitch along the translucent pipework in time to the metronomic throb-suck-throb of the machine. The students watch mesmerized as the first red worm reaches its destination and spreads out in ragged curtains down the inside of the glass drum. In fifteen minutes, the drums are quarter-full.
The tutorial is over.
With the erect professor at its head,
the chevron of origami hominids patters
through a labyrinth of lobbies and dingy corridors.
They pass a trolley-bed being pushed in the opposite direction by two male nurses in green overalls. The professor stops his group, whispers something to one of the nurses, and glances as he does so at student Forty-nine. On the trolley lies a thin man in a suit of crumpled pinstripe.
'James, me ol' pal!' chirrups Green George, 'How are we? Still lying down for the Guild, I see.'

More corridors.
Through a steel door,
guarded on both sides
by a brace of burly thugs,
gunned and truncheoned.
Some-one notices that Forty-nine has vanished.
Disquiet ripples, unobtrusively,
through the whole cortège.

Down,
deeper.
Barebrick tunnel.
Converted sewer.
Elevated walkway.
Ventilation shafts above,
a sense of rotting faeces below.

Another guarded door.
Another guarded trolley,
piled with filth, blubber.
Abel Matthews.
As they found him.
Unconscious.
The face a mask of
hard brown blood.

Ramp up to ground level...
Slap! Rubber to rubber...
The Hospital.

tab: 53

in which a boy views his fellow citizens on their way
to a most solemn occasion

Fifth day.
Early evening.
The Vintry Gardens.

'Originally used as a monks' graveyard, the area between Beadlegate and Holliwell Hill is known as Vintry, an old name derived from the Abbey Vineyards which prospered here in the twelfth and thirteenth centuries.'

DONG DONG DEDONG..........
DONG-DE DONG..........
GEDEDONG GEDEDONG GEDEDONG...

Kinch tries a second time. Reverses over pebbles and over the smooth blocks of the herringbone path, until he feels the seat of the bench once again digging into the backs of his knees.

GE DE DONG... GE DE DONG...

Off he runs, taking huge strides across the yellow brick path. With a final push he launches himself over the pebbles and onto the low-sloping trunk of the Lebanon cedar, *'Planted 1799. Gift of Isabel de Borbon'.* Three giant steps along the trunk, and then a leap forward with his arms outstretched, reaching up and high.

This time his fingers find the thick upstand of corded bark encircling the inverted armpit of the great cedar, where it splits into four.
Over the upstand. Into the hollow.

DONG DE... DONG DE...

One of the four branches
hangs parallel with the ground.
One arches out over the garden wall.
The other two rear up into the foliage,
dark, fibrous viridian, layer on layer,
pulled and flattened into claws.
He looks around.
Chooses.

DIDIDIDIDID..........
GEDOGGEDOGG-GEDEDONG..........
GEDONG GEDONG..........
GEDEDONG GONG..........
DED-O-O-O-ONG..........

Sitting astride the neck of his dendroid brontosaurus, Kinch works himself forward and upward to an outcrop of young branches. At this point he stands, weaving his way through the branchlets to a horizontal bough with a flat dipping curve, which he clears of twigs and appropriates for use as a prickly seat. Now above the wall of the Vintry Garden, he has a clear view of Augustine's Way and the Chapter House doors. Below him, through the needles, he can also see the first arrivals for tonight's big event, the Memorial High Mass Extraordinary of St. Wulfrig Obastinans.

Glasses. From pocket.

Hook them on tight.

Heads of hats and hair, grey hair, grey shoulders. Saying nothing.
Bowed. Pummelled by the bells. Alone. Twos and threes. No children.
No touching. No running. No looking up.

DONG-ONG..........

There.

Manifold Stephens, dapper-hatted Hebridean watchmaker, and Flora, his
succulent dapper-hatted wife. From Kinch's own street, 28, the small
house opposite. Kingussie Flora, always popping round for this and that,
dropping in for coffee with his mum, sparring and flirting with him. And
as for all those pointless five quid jobs around her immaculate house...
and as for her, always just stepped out of the shower with a fluffy bathrobe
clutched to her pink flesh, teasing him for his confusion... And then of
course, that time in the bus, the long journey back from Market Day in
Shipley, top deck front seat, summer-frocked thigh pressed hotly to his,
hands fluttering over his, darting little squeezes to knees and forearm,
sharing her expensive butterscotch.

Into the porch they go.

DONG-ONG..........

There.

Good old Eeny. Enoch Bangs and his lifelong anonymous miserable
girlfriend. Flatcap Eeny, fast bowler, slogger, resident foul-tempered
rough diamond fixture of the Farmtown Cricket Club. A 'card'. Well
loved by all. But not Kinch. Not by Kinch, who try as he might,

cannot forget last summer being trapped with two other boys in the cricket club toilets by this good old lovable son-of-a-gun institution and made to look on as he rubbed his gigantic forty-year-old purple-veined cock to nauseating efflorescence. Good old Eeny.
Into the porch.

DONG-ONG...........

And there.
Idris 'Sheepshagger' Crump and his wife Bronwyn, awesome oligarchs of Kinch's junior school. Administrators of their own stern brand of biblical socialism. Disciplinarians of the old kidney. And those assemblies. Sheepshagger at the lectern, booming out the laws of Marx and Moses, surveying his mystified pupils benignly over the rim of his heavy bi-focals. And on a table to his left, an umbrella rack displaying a row of twelve canes, taxonomically arranged according to weight, length, efficacy. And seated to his right, at another table, Bronwyn Crump, deputy head, 'The Train', solid and powerful, needing no threat of birchwand or hellfire to fill the children under her tutelage with diarrhoeic dread. Kinch stays very still as they stroll beneath him, at a carefully respectable distance behind the malodorous Eeny Bangs.
Into the porch.

DONG-ONG...........

In clusters they drift past, suited, dour, even the most wayward co-opted into a state of crypto-decency by the grimness of the occasion.

There, trimmed and tuckered by experts, go the Leaches, partners in
borderline jiggery-pokery, often in court but never sent down, and never
failing to embarrass Kinch with a grin, a knowing wink to a fellow scamp.
With their mother.
Into the porch.

DONG-ONG..........

And there the Clacks, wheybrained over-the-fence neighbours from
six years back, before the move to the flat. He wonders what their
son Colin looks like now. Would they recognise each other?
And there, Kip Smith, mobile fishmonger,
hung like a horse, they say,
pokes like a pony, they say.
By himself for once.

And the Wheelers. And the Wilsons.
And Doctor Zack, his first doctor,
who pulled the big red crayon
from his nose all those years ago.
People from shops, street people.
Faces with no name.

DONG-ONG..........

So many.
Why so many?
Perhaps his...
No no...

But so many.
And now...
It can't be...

DONG-ONG..........

Maeve and Stevie. A surprise. He knows they come every Sunday, but why now? As they pass underneath, he blows a hiss. Maeve looks up, frowns, then smiles. A verger on porch duty spots him, and disappears inside. 'Trouble,' mutters Kinch, as he begins the difficult return journey.

Halfway down, backwards, astride the saurian neck,
the Lady Chapel door squeaks open.
Then another noise. Nasal canine.
'Oi! You! Down!'
He twists round, to see the verger, an old enemy,
swaying from side to side with anticipatory relish,
clutching a bamboo cane.

At last he reaches the cupped platform at the top of the massive trunk. The black-suited predator is still down below, waiting for him. One foot rests on the flank of Kinch's tree. The hands grip the cane at either end, flexing it over his knee. The boy turns to the lowest and narrowest of the four main branches, the one running parallel to the ground. He takes the run in long light steps, putting as little weight as possible on the branch. The bark is smooth like skin, but he doesn't slip.
The verger crashes through the pebbles behind him.
A bough, a spiky upright, lurches towards him.

Without slowing,
he leaps left,
into air...

He lands on pebbles,
and stumbles and falls
forward onto his palms and
scrambles up onto the path
in one unbroken movement.

A sprint for the open doorway of the garden wall.
Through the door. Out into the street.
A steady jog through the alleyways of Old Axton.
Until he's safe.
Safe.

Safe.

tab: 54

which documents the shockingly blasphemous undermining of the very last
High Mass Extraordinary to be held in the Abbey Cathedral

Fifth day,
da capo...
early evening...

'- not seen -'

'- not seen -'

'- not seen -'

Among the first arrivals,
Maeve and Stevie enter the Chapter House, take a schedule from the
ever-simpering off-the-peg curate, and then turn left under an Early
Norman arch. Stevie reaches out to stroke the limestone architrave.
Celtic circles. Sooty Tudor roses.
Before her, in the fading light,
glints the cut pomegranate
of the North Transept Window.

They follow their co-pilgrims through the Abbott's Door, between the
tombs of two local hermits, Roger of Markyate, who was mentor to the
anchoress Christina, and Sigar of Northaw, who walked eight miles
daily to the service at the Abbey and is said to have banished nightingales
from Northaw because they disturbed his meditation.

And now left again, down the South Choir aisle and into the Great
Nave, third longest in England, where they take their usual chairs,
towards the back. Stevie rests her shoulder against the piped marble

of a Middle English column. From here they have an unimpeded view of the original twelfth-century Norman pilasters. Square-sectioned, thrown together with bricks looted from the derelict Roman Hypocaust, the rough columns were then plastered over and the still-damp plaster adorned with frescoes by the Head Painter and his assistants, using earth pigments bound with skimmed milk. On the outer side of each pilaster lingers the red and black palimpsest of a standardized early saint. On the well preserved more inward-facing sides however, a ragbag of hot-headed apprentices have each painted their own quirky notion of their celebrated Redeemer's protracted demise.

Beyond the nearest of the frescoed arches, in the North Choir aisle, stands all that remains of the Shrine of St. Wulsig, a rickety pedestal of stanchions and spires and ornately carved folklore,
which once,
once,
once...

> '...And we saw them deface the monuments of the dead, break open the graves and burn the bones, and we saw them rip out the brasses, and tear down the achievements and canopies from the tombs. And into their rough wagons were thrown chalices, ewers, silver candlesticks, marble statues, costly drapes and altarcloths.'

once...

> 'And as we looked on, the soldiers laughed at us and shewed us our white faces in plates of polished gold.'

once...

'And because I had not seen my reflection before,
I ran trembling from that place.'

which once...
which once sheltered,
beneath a damask awning,
the jewelled reliquary of the Saint –
once –
once –
once –

And beyond the Shrine,
the Watching Chamber...

The aunts are early.
The Choir Stalls are empty.
Empty, that is, except
for a motionless soutaned figure seated in a dark corner,
hidden from the sisters by the lampshade of an electric candle.
Watford Scales. Growing a beard it seems, and attempting to memorise
a passage of text from a book not thick enough to be the Bible.
The chairs start to fill up, from the front.
The organ booms out a heavy chord.
The tune starts well enough
but degenerates
to a plaintive leer.

A bald man in a bright blue sweater
hangs a wooden hymn board
below the fresco of Saint Blaise,
and limps off.
Split-Lipped Louie, the Cathedral mascot.

Friends nod to friends.
On arrival, all
but the very old
kneel and pray.
The organ dies.

A voice.
Singing.
From somewhere.

From somewhere deep inside the building.
A razorblade alto soaring upward
against logic and gravity. Swallow-winged. Effortless.
Other voices join in, suborning the first to regimens of hierarchy, shape,
order. Twin gates open in the roodscreen and extrude, in two identical
strands, sixteen singing choirboys, each apparelled in a long scarlet robe
buttoned all the way up from the floor to the white radiating pleats of a
daisy-wheel choker. They take their places in opposing stalls and
continue singing *a-cappella* until the Choirmaster arrives and instates
himself centrestage with his back to the assembled worshippers.
And raises his hands.
The singing stops.

A priest, whom the sisters recognise as the Dean, walks to the central lectern and welcomes the congregation, swollen now to about four hundred by Maeve's reckoning.

The Choirmaster drops his hands.

Choir and organ elbow their way into Psalm 31.

Verse after verse of sterile piety. At last it finishes.

All stand, for the first hymn, *'Lord, enthroned in Heavenly Splendour'.*

All sit. The Dean reads the first lesson, Ezekiel.

Stand. Another hymn. *'God has gladdened... etc....'*

Anthem and refrain.

Bored by all this,

Maeve regards her co-religionists.

Two rows in front of her, a fat-necked man in a sports jacket is fidgeting, discreetly. Ants are the problem, crawling from the pores of his skin and colonising his underwear. Near him Maeve recognises and nods to one of the regulars, a showy greasy baritone, moustachioed in yellow cup handles and appendaged by his pony-tailed wife who always comes with him and always sits resolutely silent with hands in pockets throughout the whole standing sitting kneeling communion-receiving protocol.

All sit.

The Dean gathers his papers.

In the same row as herself and Stevie, Maeve notices, not for the first time, a man in tortoiseshell half-glasses bent over a notebook, writing. He stands when the congregation stands and sits when it sits. When not writing he scrutinises his surroundings over the brink of his spectacles with what appears to be undisguised contempt. As the Dean leaves the lectern and Watford Scales glides over from the Choir Stalls to take his place, the pen slips from the writer's fingers and clatters through the holes of an iron floorgrill. Scales frowns and casts a look of wounded forbearance in the noise's general direction. The fat-necked man thinks the look is aimed at him, and at that very moment the troublesome ants start popping out all over his scalp, wriggling and rummaging among the sensitive follicles. He rubs, stabs with his fingertips, but the itching gets worse. The man at the lectern marks all this with increasing displeasure.

A guttural moan from somewhere behind them causes Maeve and her neighbours to look round. Four rows back, end chair, sits a tall pallid hunchback in a black homburg muttering incantations to himself, slumped sideways on his seat over a ravaged concertina briefcase. His hands wander all over his unshaven face in small washing movements, intermittently shielding his eyes in a gesture of utter wretchedness and despair. Unaware of the disturbance he is causing, he pulls from his bag a sheaf of badly photocopied Hebrew text and reads from it, aloud, tracking line by line with his finger.
Armageddon. Any minute.
Too much.
Scales nods to a group of vergers in the South Choir aisle, who surround and remove the unhappy semite, roughly, two per arm, others following behind with hat and case and dropped papers.

'Poor old boy,' whispers Maeve to her sister.
But Stevie is looking elsewhere...
Beyond the Shrine and rising well above it looms the Watching Chamber, or Feretory Loft, a lengthy windowed balcony of crudely fashioned oak, overhanging and supported by a room-high double cabinet, and accessed by an enclosed spiral staircase. Usually the door to the staircase is open,

with a crimson rope hung between the jambs, but today, although the rope is there, the door is closed. From the windows of the Loft, the pre-Dissolution monks, headed by the Custos Feretri, Keeper of the Relics, would maintain a constant watch on the Shrine and its bejewelled reliquary as queues of awestruck pilgrims lit their candles and filtered through. In the cupboards below were kept the other Relics, the Relic Authentic of the bottled mashed brain of Gereint of Rhos, the Relics Doubtful, the Relics Apocryphal, and also the more expensive Vestments...

The focus of Stevie's attention is a segment of ectoplasmic grey in a bottom corner of the central window of the Watching Chamber. As she looks, it swells and contracts like a breathing organism. Maeve follows her sister's gaze, and then she too sees it. When they stand for the next hymn, it ducks out of sight. But halfway through the second verse it reappears, grows larger, and suddenly jerks upward to reveal the bony forehead and sunken eyes of some mannish creature in torment. 'Custos Feretri!' exclaims Stevie, clutching her sister's coat-sleeve. 'Custos Feretri Turrentine, I think, dear,' whispers Maeve. 'What's he doing up there?'

Beneath a limp pasty of a hat,
the whole of Brownie's face rises into view,
finger to pursed lips, phyz bisect.
And then the entire apparition
recedes into the shadows.

The congregation sits.
Scales returns to the Choir Stalls.

The organ eases itself into
the tonic semblance of a drum roll,
and all turn right as a phantasm of gold
and purple and bright liquid carmine
ascends the twisting staircase of the High Pulpit.
The lights dim to nearly nothing.
A single powerful spotlight finds its target.

The Archbishop.
A gangling mitred greybeard in a funnel-sleeved robe of embroidered silk. Cheeks rouged, jowls aflow, he towers over his dark parishioners like a ship's figurehead. The arms unfurl, spreading wide to make a cross with his golden mitre, and then hinge forward, palms downturned, in a pass of caressing benevolence. 'Let us give praise,' he commences, 'blessed lambs of Constantine. Let us honour the Lord our God in silence for one minute, reflecting as we do so on the depth of our unworthiness.' The jowls judder. The long-nailed hands glide together. The flock kneels. For one interminable minute.

'For Yours is the Kingdom, the Power and the Glory. Amen.'
'Amen,' echoes the flock, reseating itself.

'We are here on this day to remember and to hope. To remember the glorious martyrdom of our great founder and paradigm, Saint Wulfrig Obastinans, known to heretic outsiders for so many centuries as the MerPriest of Axton, but known to his beloved disciples and fellow monks as Wulfrig the Wise. And to hope, to hope that like him we may find Eternal Peace by way of the Paths of Probity and the Strait Gate of Suffering. The miracle of Saint Wulfrig's story is known to us all, but to keep his memory ever vital we offer up, as lowly insects, this Special Mass of Celebration, every year on the sixth Friday following that First and Greatest Passion, the Passion of Christ the Redeemer.' The arms stretch forward in a double-handed hitlerian salute. 'Remember once more, dear brethren. Remember how, as a humble monk of Christ, our Saint was accused of witchcraft by the Council of Heresy, and was tried without evidence, and was tortured, and was finally submitted to the Ordeal of Water.

'O Children of Axton, abject of the Earth, why do we remember?'
'Lest we should forget, Beloved Archimandrite.'

'See him with the eyes of your mind. See him scourged with the chains of steel and stretched on the rack of wood. See him bound to the Chair of Immersion, plunged into the river for one whole hour, before being raised up and pronounced Mortuus Innocens by the Inquisitor.

'O Children of Axton, abject of the Earth, why do we remember?'
'Lest we should forget, Beloved Archimandrite.'

'Remember how the unfounded malice of his high-born accusers caused him to be cast back and left for carrion on the cold riverbed for three whole days, still tied to the terrible Chair, and how on the third day they brought him to the shore and, lo, he breathed again and stood up in a shaft of Divine Light and spake a blessing unto his tormentors.

'O Children of Axton, abject of the Earth, why do we remember?'
'Lest we should forget, Beloved Archimandrite.'

'Remember how all who saw fell prostrate at his feet and gloried in the Miracle and called him Prophet and caused him to be made Hierarch of all the South, and how in the thirty-six years of his devout and blameless ministry he built our great Abbey Cathedral, performed many miracles of healing, and converted the whole of this region to the Way of Christ and the Law of Constantine.

'O Children of Axton, abject of the Earth, why do we remember?'
'Lest we should forget, Beloved Archimandrite.'

'Remember how in his sixtieth year the soldiers of the king once again arrested him, and he was scourged once again, and was stretched on the rack once again, and was murdered once again.

'O Children of Axton, abject of the Earth, why do we remember?'
'Lest we should forget, Beloved Archimandrite.'

'Remember how, as the two-headed axe cut through his holy neck, straightway a cut appeared in the neck of his executioner, and as our Martyr's head touched the ground, so did the axeman's own head fall to the ground; and there was so much gushing blood that our river ran red for three whole days.

'O Children of Axton, abject of the Earth, why do we remember?'
'Lest we should forget, Beloved Archimandrite.'

'And remember how, when the grieving Bishops prepared and cleansed his body for the Holy Rites of Burial, lo, they found the gills of a fish at the nape of his neck and the webbed fins of a fish at the toes of his feet.

And thus they fell to the ground and once again gave thanks to Almighty God for the Wondrous Mysteries of His Ineffable Presence.

'So may the Blood of the Martyrs nourish the minutes and the days of our lives. And may the example of Saint Wulfrig be always before us. May the scourge that laid bare the bones of Axton's Martyr fall on our own flesh until our monstrous sins are bled clean and the last foul drop of pus from our cowardly hearts has dried to dust, and may that same abominable dust blow up to blind the eyes of all blasphemers.

'May the example of Saint Constantine be also and always before us. May we too be prepared to make the ultimate sacrifices, the subtraction of a lascivious wife, the abrogation of an ungrateful son. For we declare that the truest test of Gentleness is Strength. For Gentleness without Strength is as the softening of a biscuit in the Waters of Enfeeblement.

'May the example of Christ Crucified be also and always before us. Now let us kneel to remember once again Christ Our Lord's Holy Passion, closing our eyes as we consider the meaning of the nails.'
The congregation unsettles, stirs, and sinks forward.

'May we now be prepared to suffer, in company with Him.
For the greatest teacher is suffering. And love is not love without pain, for just as flame need its kindling, so does love need its lash; and thus our true and passionate love for the Son of God starts only as we enter with the soldier's spear into the Bloody Portal of His Holy Side.

'And now, in the eye of our mind, let us picture the nails.
Behold! They are huge, like iron wedges, strong enough to bear the

254

weight of a fully grown man. It is said twelve blows of the hammer are needed for each one. See how roughly and quickly the work is done. Come. Draw close to the Cross. See, He is fixed now. He can move neither Hand nor Foot and by that immobility is atoning for all the liberty we lavish on ourselves. And so with Christ must you be nailed to the Cross. What does this mean? It means your hands nailed so that all the work they do is done for Him alone. It means your feet nailed together to stop them fleeing from the rigours of His service. It means your eyes nailed through so they see nothing but Him in all His creatures. It means your ears nailed through so they hear only His commands. It means your tongue nailed to its palette so that it says nothing against His wishes. It means your flesh with all its desires, nailed and treated as dead, your intellect nailed through in its determination to know nothing but Christ Crucified, your heart so pierced with the nails of His love that it is given entirely to Him, and your will so nailed to His that it moves only in unison with Him. And thus we implore Thee, O patient pitying Christ, enclose all our senses, all the affections of our soul in Thy Sacred Wounds, that we may be joined to Thy Sacred Heart by a Great and Everlasting Destiny.

'And now be seated, and bow your sinful heads in silent prayer before the Redemptive Agonies of Wulfrig our Saint and Christ our Saviour.'

The stricken worshippers grope in the half-darkness,
fumble their way backwards onto their hard chairs.
Maeve steadies her sister, grabbing the older woman's arm
as she totters and nearly falls.

The Nave re-settles.
Heads incline again.

255

Eyelids close again.
Hands join again.
Silence.

In his exalted eyrie, the Archbishop steps back. Seats himself on a
narrow cornerstool. The spotlight dims. The organ mumbles to itself.
He reaches forward beneath the lectern and switches off the fixed
microphone. Opens a small cupboard in the oak panelling. Takes out a
mini-mike, which he clips onto his embroidered orphrey, and also two
small bladders of blood-filled polythene, which he attaches like blisters
to the palm of each hand.

A sudden chord, G-major,
clashes wall against wall.
The Nave reopens its eyes.
The Archbishop rises and is immersed in a shimmer of saffron.
Squinting against the light and seemingly in a trance, he floats down
the staircase onto the stone floor and moves forward along the
Central Aisle until he is level with the first row of seated worshippers.
The long body is rigid,
fists against thighs,
head held high.
The arms crank out to horizontal.
The sleeves hang down in golden torrents.
The wrists swivel, thumbs uppermost.

Meanwhile,
crouched in a corner
of the Watching Chamber,

Brownie directs a narrow torchbeam
across a keyboard control panel.

The archiepiscopal fists slowly uncurl:
'eeeeeeeeeeEEEEEEAAAAAAARRH!'

The noise brings Brownie to his feet.
From behind a carved mullion he sees the Archbishop held motionless
in a column of light, mouth wide open as the screech and its
disembodied litter careen and disperse through the vaulted gloom. The
priestly fingertips detach from their palms to reveal in the centre of each
priestly hand the ragged dribbling mouth of a new wound.

For one moment, Brownie, even he, is beset by doubts.
Three women in the congregation faint outright and are stretchered
away by soutaned orderlies who materialise silently from the shadows.
Maeve and Stevie are clutching hands, not looking, heads bowed.

For minutes after the screech has died away
its memory plays and replays inside Brownie's head.

Through all of this, the Archbishop stands statued, cruciform.
But now he turns and turns again, in two complete rotations.
Mouth closes. Breath deepens. Nostrils gape.
The mouth re-opens, this time to speak.
The jowls. The long stained teeth.
Him. It can only be him.
Brownie returns to his control panel.

'O Almighty Christ, my Sweetest Love,' the clanging bell of the priest's voice rings out, 'inflame this fickle heart of mine, that it may be always and all on fire for Thee. And therefore let us be at one with the ardent petition of Saint Augustine:-

O Lord, may I know myself and know Thee
And desire nothing save only Thee;
May I do everything for Thy sake,
May I be poor for the sake of Thee,
May I hate myself and love Thee,
May I die to myself and live in Thee.'

From the organ
comes a weak lament, like a leaking cyst...

The Archpriest's hands move inward to smear the blood all over his face.
Watford Scales approaches and presents his superior with a heavy glass amphora filled with purple wine.
The priest takes a lengthy sip
and raises it above his head.
'Blood of Wulfrig, inebriate me.'
DO-NNNNG...
From above, an F-sharp, struck low...
then lost in the marrow of the walls.
He drinks again.
'Blood of Wulfrig, inebriating chalice, intoxicate my heart with Divine Adoration for my Creator, my Blessed Redeemer and Spouse of my soul.'
DO-NNNNG...
Drinks again.
'Blood of Wulfrig, inebriating chalice, wine that makes virgins, permeate my body with the gift of Holy Purity.'

DO-NNNNG...
Gulp.
'Blood of Wulfrig, celestial ichor, inundate my soul with an avid desire
to embrace all the sufferings which the Lord God may send me.'
DO-NNNNG...

DO-NNNNG...

DO-NNNNG...

He passes the amphora to Scales and once again raises his arms to
display to the packed Cathedral the crushed tulips of his stigmata.
'Now of thee, Wulfrig, Saint of Axton, we beg for grace in pain: by the
blood which flowed under the burning smart of thy scourging, by the
blood which spurted from the joints of thy holy limbs as they suffered
and split on the abominable rack, by the blood which washed over thy
holy feet and poured from thy sacred neck at the crime of thy beheading.'
Scales hands back the half-empty amphora to his Archbishop,
who once more raises it above his upturned face.

'Blood of Wulfrig, baptize me.'
The amphora tilts back.
A trickle of wine splashes onto his forehead
and streams down his bloodied cheeks.

'Blood of Christ and Wulfrig, blind me.'
Without warning,
the spotlight dims, and all the other lights fail completely.
The priest has his eyes shut against the wine, sees nothing.
The congregation stirs only slightly.

'Blood of Christ and Wulfrig, drown me.'
Above the priest, on a partially restored
blank section of the rood screen,
appears a rectangle of light
the size of a small bus.
'Blood of Christ, anoint me,' he continues.
'Blood of Christ... Blood of Christ... Blood of... Blood of... Chr...'

Something strange is happening to his voice.
It is meandering, stumbling, getting lost in a kind of aural fog,
and through the fog comes another, higher, voice to take its place.
'False Priest! Liar Priest!' blazons the new voice, over and over.
'Liar Priest! Liar Priest! Charlatan! Hypocrite!
You have deceived and betrayed us all!'

The Archbishop staggers back, blinking, blinded by wine.
The amphora slips from his hands and shatters on the floor.

'Priest?' declaims the voice. 'This is no priest. Look at him. This is
Admetus, you poor fools! Admetus, the corrupt professor. Admetus,
the defiler of women. Harold Admetus, the degenerate bully whose
crimes have for decades been protected by the Abbey Guild.
Regard your *'Beloved Archimandrite'*!'

The mitre topples from the priest's head and releases a cascade of silver
hair. Even in this dim light the shape of the man's head is unmistakeable.
The sound of his name hisses around the Nave like a fly caught in a fist.
At a sign from Scales, a dozen black vergers appear out of nowhere and
surround the lurching figure.

'And now, look up! Look up at the rood screen!' commands the new voice as the last rays of the spotlight fade. 'This is your Archbishop! This is your true Wall of Blood! Look up! Look up!'

The loudspeakers splutter.

The oblong of light on the crucifixion fresco becomes a cinema screen, a box of grainy rain. The rain melds into angles and the angles harden into the corner of a bare room. A cry, female, off camera. The sound of a struggle. Men's voices. The face of Admetus, beaded with sweat, floats in from the right and leads the camera across a tiled floor to where a naked woman is being strapped by the wrists and ankles to a low wooden pallet. Four men in suits, one at each corner, doing the work. Admetus, in a dressing gown, holding a coiled whip, watching, directing. The cycle tracks of a previous whipping are all over her. The camera moves briefly to her face, a shell of terror but unmarked and evidently East Asian, and then across the flogged breasts, and up along an arm to a bound wrist. The film slows to quarter-speed. The image moves jerkily and the voices deepen to a jungle roar. Male fingers force open the small red hand and place the point of a steel tent-peg against the palm. Zoom out. Admetus. Bent forward. Over her. Raising a hammer. Driving the nail home.

The image blacks out.
The lights come on.

The screams start.

A few of the congregation are clambering over chairs in a noisy rush towards the Chapter House. Some are stumbling around the Nave,

261

half-blind, nonplussed. Some are looking upward, mouthing prayers. A dozen are converging angrily on Admetus. But most remain paralysed in their places.

Where is it coming from, the screaming? There. In the Lady Chapel. Four young ordinands have collapsed onto the floor in a shared fit and are rolling about the aisle, knocking into each other, howling uncontrollably.

Admetus is being held by Scales and the vergers. His face is a butcher's block of blood and wine-drool and melting make-up. He seems stupefied by the alcohol and offers no objection as they drag him backwards to the presbytery. Hands reach out to tear the vestments from his body. Tassels are ripped from his orphrey. The purple stole is pulled from under his cope and trampled into the ground. The fat-necked man in the sports jacket, no longer troubled by ants, has worked his way through the crowd. He leaps forward, throws a fist over the vergers' heads and lands it on the point of his Archbishop's nose. Gristle gives. Blood pours.

Split-Lipped Louie rocks to and fro, sucking the blue out of his sleeve.

The door of the Watching Chamber opens. Brownie Turrentine bursts out, still holding his torch, features twisted in rage and disgust as he pushes through the crowd. 'You lazy fools!' His actor's voice booms over everything. 'When will you wake up? When will you ever learn?' Before the Chapter House entrance, he leaps onto the bookstall, scooping up handfuls of books and papers and pamphlets

which he hurls, salvo on salvo, high into the consecrated air.
'Wake up, you children, and face yourselves!
This isn't just a harmless daydream.
It's killing people! It's always killed people!'

He catches sight of Maeve and Stevie,
holding each other, weeping.

He turns away, jumps down,
capsizes the bookstall, and stalks out
through the Chapter House Door.

tab: 55

...the jade monkey's last tale,

concerning Craftsmanship and The Law.

"A poor knifegrinder of Ch'u once read in the Book of Science and Learning: 'The mantis preys on the cicada from behind a leaf that renders him invisible.' With this in mind, he searched the bushes near his house and, sure enough, soon espied a mantis holding out such a leaf in readiness for a passing cicada. Beside himself with joy, he grabbed the leaf and ran to the marketplace. With his leaf held out before him, he began stealing all manner of goods in full view of the astonished stallholders. He was at once arrested by the market guards and hauled before the magistrate, who listened carefully to the man's story, burst out laughing, and ordered both arms to be cut off at the elbow. The nearest guard drew his sword, but, being slightly deaf, and, as he admitted later, slightly drunk on homemade huang-jiu,
cut the man's head off by mistake.
'Ssss... Ssss... Ssss...
Ssss.. some sharp sword!'
the head exclaimed admiringly,
as it rolled across the floor..."

tab: 56

in which Kaisa cooks a meal

Skewbald.
Studying him,
over the rim of her goblet.

'What do you think, young man?'
'Very nice.' He stares around him, at the room, at the quiet surface of
his wine, the pictures on the wall, postcards, unframed reproductions,
'*The Two Travellers*' by Jack Yeats, W.B.'s younger brother.
'That's how memories are,' he says.
'Broken. In pieces.'

'Maybe,' she frowns, rolling the stem
between her thumb and forefinger.
'For me, it's always changing.
So many possibilities. D'you... ?'
He frowns back. 'I don't know. Maybe.'

House spider, leg-span two inches,
female *tegenaria gigantea*,
pictograms down its back,
crossing the carpet.

'How's the arm?'
'A lot better thanks.'
'Must have been awful.'

'I feel bad about it. The dog... dogs. They're just animals. They're not really... not difficult. Not like people.'

She sits down beside him, on the sofa.

'People in general?'

'People in general. Though I'm better with women.'

He reddens. 'You're the only one I'm scared of.'

She takes his arm, adjusts the bandage.

Look, look about, Pigeon.

The pictures...

'What's that? With the running bull and the strange dancers?'

'From Crete. Bull-leaping, they call it. As if life wasn't hard enough in those days. Bulls were sacred to the Minoans. Smaller than our modern ones. The bulls, that is. And their horns were blunted. Still... Somersaulting over a charging bull... Makes you think, doesn't it?'

For some reason or reasons entirely obscure to himself, he bursts into laughter, too loud, and is about to attempt suitably obscure clarification when the doorbell and the oven-timer ring at the same time. She goes to the kitchen to adjust the oven and he shambles out to the hall door. A dishevelled, grinning and somewhat breathless Kinch stands there, looking up at him. 'I was just passing. Thought I'd see if you were here.' Kaisa joins them. 'You'd better come in,' she sighs in mock irritation. 'It so happens we're about to eat. Should you by any chance be hungry, there's enough for three.'

'No, I'm fine thanks.'

'Really? Come in and sit yourself down. Next to Piet.'

'Piet?'

'Pigeon. From now on it's Piet. Ok?'

He looks over her shoulder
at the man in question,
who gives him a wink.

At the table, waiting for food,
Kinch runs his fingers over the ridged landscape of the tablecloth,
constructs Martian deathray tripods with the Scandinavian cutlery.
Pigeon looks on.

'Been here before then?'
'Couple of times. Do I really have to call you Piet?'
'No-no. Pigeon's fine. Where've you...?'
'The Cathedral. Up the big tree. Loads of people, going to the Mass.'
'Interesting?'
'Not very.'
'Well, it certainly looks like you've had an interesting time. How
about tidying yourself up a bit?'
Pigeon hands him a comb.
The boy shrugs, accepts it,
and saunters off to the bathroom.

Kaisa returns with a steaming casserole
which she places gingerly on the table.
'Not what I had in mind exactly,' she smiles.
'Kaisa?'
'Mm?'
'It's good you have your own name for me. I like it. But please don't
ask others to... you know...'
'Ok. We still going to London next month?'

'I'm looking forward to it.'

'I was thinking, of...' she begins, her gaze intently on him, 'of asking Kinch if he'd like to come along, before he goes back to school. Would you mind? He's gone through a lot, and his mum is on such a knife-edge.'

'No, of course not. Good idea.'

A combed and renovated Kinch emerges,
reseating himself next to Pigeon,
who asks, 'How's your mum?'
'Alright,' he replies, staring hard
at an exhibition poster, on the wall.
Monet's 'Waterloo Bridge, Grey Day'.

Kinch is dreaming.
Dreaming his way
through a blizzard
of paint and steam.

Kaisa touches the boy's shoulder.
'It's been hard for her,' she says.

'Yeah...
I know.'

Pigeon clears his throat.
'Ever been to London, Kinch?'
No response.

'Kinch?'

tab: 57

in which a rolling stone stops rolling

Day six.

Mid-morning.

Tiger Street.

Saturate articulating light floods in through the cartwheel window onto an antique wind-up easel, set as close to the window as the sloping attic ceiling will allow. Facing it, propped against the chest of drawers, is a head-to-toe mirror detached from the fitted wardrobe, and next to that a long-legged glass-topped palette table, rimmed with fresh worm-casts, in order, dark to bright to white, oil-ground pigment. A tall shape moves into radiance, clamps canvas to easel, shuffles round the room, takes a brush in one hand and a rag in the other, stares at the floor, stares at the mirror.

Brownie. Artist. Laired,

stalking essence, the fabled centre.

Now. Begin.

Peach black, titanium, raw sienna.

Cone on cone. Hair in umber talon over right eye, point held in triangle of light, sharded orange, all down the left fall. Blueblack shadow before the streamline edge of bone cheek chin. Nose in a knuckle down to cleft hexagon tip. Brows fork from bridge, arms of flying fox. One soft black iris, poised in a beano bomb, the other dropping low, soft black yoke in shiny sac, pulling low on its latex lid.

As he looks and looks again, the cheek ignites from slugskin to hot ochre. The brush draws and redraws the cone-on-cone of head and hair, the tilted square potato of face and jaw. Too small. Too large.
Head and loose-shirted trunk twist in opposite directions.

The wall behind him is littered all over with wigs and hats and the tools of his former occupation. Too much. Downs brush. Drags a khaki blanket off the bed and hangs it hook-to-hook over the whole caboodle. Returns to the mirror, shaken by the rupture, the figure's isolation.

Number eight hogshair. Gather white and black and flowerpot red. Spatter in oblique abaxial sprawl across brow nose and cheek. Scrape it on scrape it off. Mix drift of dun mortar on the glass palette. Reconstruct the double cone, finding and describing a vertical folding pattern where the light passes left to right across hair face shoulder hair.
And, ah...
but the light changes, as an indigo nazi thunderbolt zigzags down eyebrow and overhung socket. And as the light changes, he changes.

Step back. See the background. Huh! With a two-inch housepainter's brush he slashes khaki round the head and shoulders, losing the hair. Dropping brush to ground, he attacks the canvas with a rag-covered fist, searching again for pattern as light strafes the facetted cutglass meat.

The head grows. The hours pass.
The gridded square transcodes from rainbow chaos into blood and lungs and rock. Unbandaged. Torn-apart. Refigured.
Bled and born.

And so he rides the dragon...
he, Sinbad Brownie, soaring through climates of the upper air, for whole
minutes at a time breaking into that self-destroying bliss of concentration
which delivers the best work at the critical time, sliding off and diving
down through leaves of poison to spinneys of lead, of despair, to grow
antlers, to be savaged by his own dogs, to be sucked out sideways, to join
battle hand-to-hand with the mutating chimaeras of Cud and Praxis.

Nothing like it.
No other thrill, no exaltation, compares with this.
So how will he, how can he possibly notice
that other presence in the room?

How will he hear the creaking of the boards
when all he hears is the beating of his dragon's wings?

How will he see the edge of the mirror's field
irrupted by the shoulder and then the hood
of an olive duffle-coat, when all he sees
is the jet of blue dragonflame
scorching paths, welding continents
across the sprung belly of his canvas?

Even the telephone-cable
garrotte about his throat will
feel like nothing more than
another beast of misprision
to cut down and cut out
on this high day of chivalry.

Only when his brushes
and his knives hit the floor,
and his head is jerked back
to meet the cold
forget-me-not gaze
of Clarissa Mockhardt,

will he realise
that something

is most seriously

                    up.

tab: 58

which is the last appearance of Clarissa and the Dean

Shadows, stableyard,
on the mauve cobbles,
shadows of the palace,
on the phaeton's passenger,
shadows of the palace,
and a clammy rigour.

Nervous he is,
as only she can make him.
A pair of StigSoc grooms are hitching up the horses when he catches
sight of her poppies-on-turquoise bolero flashing through the aspens
and the cobalt skirtpleats swinging to the rhythm of her stride.
Duffle-coat over arm.
Clarity.

'Dump it,' she clips, handing the coat to one of the grooms. Ignoring the
mounting block, she sweeps round to the back of the phaeton and hauls
herself up using the suspension bar as footrung. The chassis rocks in its
harness. She looks down at him. Disdain. Cut with something else.
'That's it. In future you dogs of the Guild can do your own dirty work.'
'He's dead then?'
'What do you think?'
'Dead then.'

The grooms,
thankyousir,
have finished.

She takes the reins,
quickens to the smell of leather,
the theatre of muscle-racked horsehide.
'Come on, sweet ladies. Let's go.'

The mares tremble,
clatter their burden
into the sun.

tab: 59

in which Pigeon and Kaisa seek sweet convergence

Day seven.
Farmtown Square.
Early afternoon. The Old Town Hall,
a three-sided three-legged redbrick husk, used for most of its postwar
life as inadequate fire station, and before that, in its now-derelict upper
room, as inadequate Council Chamber. Of the three ground floor
arches which until recently gave access to Farmtown's weekly market,
two have been bricked up and footed with long oak benches, while the
third has a gate which opens every Friday to accommodate the mobile
shop of McMurty & Son, Yarmouth fishmonger.

Pigeon. Sitting in the sun, on one of the long benches.
A warm breeze carries with it the smell of aged wetfish, infolded with
another smell, the smell of aged fagsmoke, currently billowing from the
aged lungs of Mrs Mother-of-McMurty, seated, turbaned, bronchitic,
on the other end of his bench.
People pass by with their shopping.
He looks straight at them, coldly,
eye to eye, for the first time it seems.
A few stare back, turn away.

Enough.
Up.
Walk on.

A ten minute walk, through the Sunday streets of Farmtown Village. Terraced cottages give way to flint walls and broadleaf hedges, to converted farm buildings, and finally to 'Hillhaven', a row of jacobean workhouses now used by the Abbey Guild as a hostel for unemployables and misfits. He looks up at the end window. No movement in the lace curtain. Home to Velma, mythic trollop-succubus of the Farmtown backalleys, favourite unmissable target of church gossip and playground wit, who'll open her legs for five and go all the way for twenty. So they say. Wears purple brocade of an evening. Made-up thick and pale, like raw piecrust.

Outsider. Friend. Argonaut.

And as he walks,

the town falls from him like a disease.

Into Hill Road.

'Hello, Kaisa.'

She is early, outside The Carter's Arms in a loose yellow dress.

'Hello, Piet.'

They move off together. The road is pavementless, empty apart from the occasional farmer's car to keep them on their toes. On one side is a thistlebank, a ditch, scrappy hedgerows, cornfields; and on the other, mown verges, lawns, clipped conifers, the detached homes of middle-order suits and Cathedral staff. Greentrees Convalescent Home slips by, shielding its face behind weeping willows and implacable chestnuts.

A big flake of slate, polished, inscribed, dangles from the gatepost of the last house – *'With the kiss of the sun for pardon, and the song of the birds for mirth, one is nearer God's Heart in a garden, than anywhere else on Earth'.* 'So I've noticed,' hisses Kaisa, glancing from the barren sanctimony of the garden in question to the view ahead, of the Hill, southside, splashed with sun, rabbled with dusty furze, with stunted, blossoming, off-kilter blackthorns. 'If I'm wrong, and there is a God, you can bet your life He, She or It doesn't hang out in an Axton front garden.'

She reaches sideways
to poke him in the ribs.
'Race you to the first stile.'
He watches as she runs ahead, sturdy over graceful, with a dancer's strength in her calves, her buttercup shift pitching in the breeze. He lollops after her, shaking the ground at each step. The path rises gradually and by the time it reaches the stile is already on the first slopes of the Hill. About to overtake, he slows and lets her win. They lean on the stile for breath. 'You win,' he says. She punches his good arm, laughing. 'You let me, you patronising rotter.'

Over the stile. Up a steep tunnel of nettle-mobbed bushes and out into a long clearing, even steeper, dotted with low gorse, wild privet, aborted rabbit warrens. Underfoot the moss-coated ground feels soft, hillocky. Next to the clearing is an immense triangle of chalk, fashioned in the 1880's by an eccentric local squire. In a splurge of Victorian zeal, he single-handedly hacked out this white isosceles in the turf by exposing, only six inches beneath the topsoil, the cracked pallor of the calcium bedrock. The 'White Mark', as it has always been known, was meant to give the illusion, when approached from the east, of an impressive steeple arising from the squat square belltower of Saint Stephen of the Hundred Arrows. In reality, of course, the daft squire's 'illusion' has never fooled anyone.

The springiness in the ground is a surprise, giving a dreamlike ease to their climb. 'Look!' she cries as a grizzled fox dashes across the White Mark and disappears into the bushes.

A couple of yards above the chalk apex they sit on a skullcap of brittle moss, looking down at the landscape far below,
towards Farmtown, Old Axton,
and the Blood Wall,
gleaming like a newbuild
in the broken brilliance.

They scan to the right, over Barley Moor, across the Marsh to the Five Men. And then left, over a lattice of cornfields to the half dozen villages which speckle the foothills of Wenlop Ridge. She points them out, names them, talks fondly of the people living there.

Butterflies dawdle and flirt. Dragonflies keep watch.
Between her sentences, the faint bass echo of traffic blends with the trill of birdsong into a hushed and sunny music. The skin of her shoulder is so smooth, so steeped through with buttery ochres that not to lean over and kiss the nearest curve of it seems an utter impossibility. She turns towards him as he does so, and kisses him on the top of his head, takes his head between her hands and kisses him softly on the lips. 'Come,' she says, 'Let's walk some more. I'm getting pins and needles.'

They meander on, weaving in silence between islands of bramble. Rabbits scamper away at every corner. He reaches for her hand. A smile sends his thoracic organs backsomersaulting into each other. And still the swelling velvet underfoot,

flecked with little nuggets of chalk,
mined and scattered by the rabbits.

He leads her down the west side of the Hill,
where the thickets are denser, taller.
They sit down to rest in a hidden glade ringed by a wall of bramble and
an inner cloister of oak and beech saplings. She takes two apples from
her tiny rucksack and hands him one. Down in the distance, a point of
sunlight on a car roof moves like a shooting star through the haze.
Harebell and wild strawberry crowd his feet. Never has apple tasted
sweeter. She throws her core into the bushes, and he does the same. She
flops back on the bed of dry grass, her mouth still wet from the juice of
the apple. He leans over and touches her lips with his. She draws him to
her and they tip sidelong in a sudden embrace.
'So, so much...,' he, weeping.
She rocks him,
kissing eyes, tears,
until he is quiet again.

Her body feels warm and strong and supple, her breasts small and soft
against him. She rolls onto her back, drawing his hand across her. And
he sees his hand, mentored by hers, now cradling, now kneading, and
then her own hand on his fly, touching, stroking. And then the buttons
of her dress, one by one, freed by her own quick fingers, down to the
hem. The dress drawn apart and the slim lovely shape of her.
Her nipples in his mouth and the taste of her.
Now, mouth to mouth, ravening.
'Kaisa, Kaisa...'
'Lie back,' she whispers.

He lies back. With the thin shift hung loosely about her, she starts to undress him. He trembles in disbelief, watching as her frock swings open, watching the honey-roast warmth of her, watching the wide smile, the moist eyes, watching as she kicks off her coral panties and then, with a reassuring grin, peels down his own blue boxer shorts. Still looking at him, she lowers her head, circles the glans with her tongue, kisses its dark eye. 'Minun...' Sheds frock. Kisses his stomach. Eases off his shirt. Kisses his lips and the carmine roughness of his birthmark, *nevus flammeus, woven fire*. She draws away, springs to her feet, spreads out frock and shirt on the hot turf, and drops down again. On her side, propped on one elbow, she reaches out to his wounded arm, touches the bandage, takes his hand, cogging fingers with his. 'Minun lemmikki...' Her hand is small and warm and dry. She pulls him to her, off the grass and onto the bed of cotton. Once more they cling to each other, flesh to flesh, never wanting it to end. He shuts his eyes to fix everything forever, and opens them to see her golden head looking up at him from the pillow of his shirt. Feels her thighs spread, the knees lift, and the legs curl around his own. Her hand slides down between their bellies, finds his cock, which seems to him incongruous and clumsy and in the way. Her fingers are on it, round it, guiding. For a while he stays still, with the head of it resting there, in the folds of her, of Kaisa, after so long; then he pushes in, gentle, and she pulls him in, and the centre pulls him in, and he knows at last, at long last, in this grass, this brief heat, this jade sun,

knows he is not, cannot be,

surely,

alone.

tab: 60

in which a boy stands on a brink

Day seven,
da capo. Old Axton.
Early afternoon. Ship Street.

Kinch.
Cool. Squashed nose.
Glass. Junkshop window.
A something, unusual, in
its usual dusty winter of
junkshop plates, eggcups,
souvenir ashtray machines,
ice and fog, decrepit cupids,
humiliated shepherdesses.

A something, unusual. An owl theme.
Hollow-eyed ceramic and sequin-eyed in brown rags,
in brass, marquetry, plaster, big-eyed, dark-eyed atavistic,
and the poems – owl poems in ugly frames, presumably composed by
the engorged starfish lady in the rear of the shop who interrupts her
composing to cast a quizzical squint in his direction. He steps back.
From an end alcove of the tableau, a real plump stuffed barn owl
surveys the poor pastiches of itself with invigilatory disdain. Kinch
edges sideways, for a closer look. To escape the woman's stare.

Though he himself is in shade
the street behind him is a river of sunlight.
Mirrored in the murk of the barn owl's niche,
people and traffic flow back and forth
through the heat, through the crackle of gold.

He tries to make out himself double-reflected in the plate mirrorglass
wall of the Axton Bank. A familiar shape catches his eye, trotting
diagonally across the street away from him. She reaches the far pavement,
seems to change her mind, stops, and walks back in the opposite
direction. He turns to greet his mother, raising a hand to wave, noting
the hard inhabited look on her face. Doesn't bother. Just watches.

She falters forward, swivels round, to check her image in the bank
wall. Then back again, towards Kinch. They look at each other, but
he knows she doesn't see him. She twists away, continues her walk.
His gullet tightens. He wants to run after her, shake her, claim
recognition. But he doesn't. Does. Doesn't.
Stomach turns cold.
Go.

Down along Trinity, dodging shoppers.
Second right, through Tin Row, under the low bridge still famously
spear-gouged by the last Henry Tudor's dissoluting horde, and out,
out into the bleak acre of Ascension Square. From here, his favoured
route, through a tangle of grim passages known as Camelot, brings
him to the re-jigged suavities of North Axton, where all roads lead to
Peter's Gate, portcullised North Barbican of the Blood Wall. Twenty
yards before Peter's Gate, he comes to the Guards' Room, padlocked,
boarded up, hidden from the street by a tiered flowerbed. He
approaches the doorway, curious.

'*GhyEEcchh!*'

The foulest stench.

Pushes hard against the rotted newly-padlocked door.

The hasp nuts give. The door scrapes open.

A dog's-head-shaped thing flops out,

matted throat-fur ticks, ripples,

churns with maggots.

Walk on.

East. Under the Wall.

Walk between. The sunny rosy marble.

The bloated ramparts of the Axton rich.

Up the ramp of Luther's Feet.

Onto the inner parapet.

Over everything.

On the Blood Wall.

These giant blocks.

Pockmarked. Worn.

But each its own colour.

He jumps down into the sentry channel

and up again onto the outer parapet.

Before his eyes the wooden watchtowers reconstruct themselves.
The Wall swarms with armed defenders. Pikemen jostle for position
in the channel. Archers kneel on the brink, awaiting the first assault.
Behind them, unarmed peasants amass piles of logs and rocks. The
first enemy catapult boulder overshoots. The second hurtles into the
legs of a watchtower, causing it to topple and crash sideways onto the
defenders. A third splinters harmlessly into the base of the Wall. The

fourth is still airborne, descending in a slow shallow curve towards a
group of women auxiliaries on their way to help at the stricken tower.
Descending...
Descending...
Blink. Delete.
Wall, empty.

He looks south, into splendour,
over treetops and the spires of the town.
Beyond. Beyond everything.
Opens himself to the artless air.
Feels the marble warming beneath his feet,
the blood pulsing through each woken block.

Looks east.
The Farm. The Hill,
hazy in the afternoon sun,
flowering, flaming, lily-tongued.
The chalkpits, no more.
The blots of gorse, gone.

· Kinch,
warm, again,
alive, in the light,
in the heat,   as

                as